For Maddie, Piper and Riley – KC

Thank you to my children, Ava and Max,
for being my inspiration – LT

STRIPES PUBLISHING
An imprint of Little Tiger Press
1 The Coda Centre, 189 Munster Road,
London SW6 6AW

A paperback original
First published in Great Britain in 2016

Text copyright © Katrina Charman, 2016
Illustrations copyright © Lucy Truman, 2016

ISBN: 978-1-84715-672-3

The right of Katrina Charman and Lucy Truman to be identified as
the author and illustrator of this work respectively has been asserted by
them in accordance with the Copyright, Designs and Patents Act, 1988.

Printed and bound in the UK.

10 9 8 7 6 5 4 3

Poppy's Place

THE HOME-MADE CAT CAFÉ

ILLUSTRATED BY
LUCY TRUMAN

KATRINA CHARMAN

Stripes

Chapter One

Isla Palmer loved cats. She loved their silky fur and little pink tongues. She loved how clever they were, and the way they purred when they were happy. But most of all, she loved how they made you feel. It was impossible to be sad when a cat was around.

Isla was sure she'd persuade her mum to let her have a cat of her very own one day. But until then, she'd just have to content herself with helping out at Abbey Park Vets, where her mum worked as a veterinary nurse. Isla liked nothing more than sitting at the front desk and meeting all the people and their pets, and it gave her the chance to snuggle with any cat who'd come in for a check-up.

Isla glanced around the surgery and smiled to herself. The summer holidays had just begun and she was looking forward to spending every possible second at the vets, allowing for maximum cat-cuddling time in between all the chores that Mum had lined up for her.

"The thing about cats," Isla said to her mum as she helped put away bandages in the supply cupboard, "is that they are so loving. Not like a hamster who would rather chew on a stick ou stroke it, or a bearded dragon who n moves and eats live bugs."

Isla's mum sighed. "The thing about cats, Isla, is that I spend all day looking after them here at work. Cleaning up their mess, feeding them, giving them stitches  after they've managed to get stuck in an old wooden fence. The last thing I need when I get home is more cats to look after."

Mum was always going on about how grown-ups didn't like to bring their work home with them. Isla couldn't understand this at all. If Mum worked in a pizza restaurant, Isla was sure that she wouldn't have a problem bringing her work home with her then.

Her mum placed the last of the bandages in the cupboard. "We've had this conversation a hundred times before, Isla. I'm sorry, but we are not getting a cat, or a stick insect, or any other type of pet. There would have to be a really good reason for me to say yes to us getting a cat – and being more loving than a bearded dragon is not a really good reason."

Isla tried to hide her disappointment. She didn't want any other type of pet. All she wanted – all she'd *ever* wanted – was a cat of her own.

"I *do* have a really good reason," Isla protested.

She searched through her backpack for her *I Heart Cats* notebook where she had written nine more really good reasons to have a cat, but before she could continue with reason number two, Mum was called away by Lucy, the vet.

Isla sighed. She should have started with something better than the loving thing. Maybe reason number six – a cat could save your life. Isla had heard about a cat who had woken its owners in the middle of the night when there had been a house fire. This was just one of the hundreds of reasons why cats were so amazing. She couldn't understand why her mum didn't feel the same.

Isla stuffed her notebook into her backpack and made her way to the holding cages behind the consulting room where they kept sick or injured animals who were recovering from a procedure or waiting to be treated. She hoped there were some cats there today.

In the first cage was Thompson –
a grumpy, overweight black Labrador who
seemed to spend more time at Abbey Park
than his own home. Mum
said he was very, very old
in dog years – almost
eighty-nine. Isla patted
Thompson's head as
he snored loudly,
and left a few
dog biscuits
for when he
woke up.

The next few cages were empty, but a
little further along, inside a glass vivarium,
was a large python called Cecil – another
regular patient – wrapped around a log.
Isla knew that snakes liked to eat frozen
mice. She shuddered, glad that she didn't

have to feed Cecil. It wasn't that she was afraid of snakes exactly, she'd just rather not touch the dead things they ate. Although Cecil didn't only eat dead things. The reason he was at the vets so often was because he was always eating things he shouldn't – this time he'd swallowed his owner's glasses. Isla thought that maybe Cecil wasn't *that* fond of dead things either.

Isla readjusted her own glasses, which had slid down her nose slightly, and went to wash her hands, thinking that there were no more animals to see. Then she heard a quiet meow coming from a cage at the end of the corridor. She hurried down to take a look. A beautiful cat sat with a thick bandage around one of its back legs. It had bright green eyes and its fur was mostly black, with white paws like little socks and a furry white chest.

Unusually, there was no name on the chalkboard outside the cage. It only said *Nil by Mouth* which meant that the cat wasn't allowed anything to eat or drink as it had either just had an operation or was about to have one. Isla gave the cat a wistful look, holding her hand up against the bars. The cat batted its front paw in the air as though it was trying to give her a high-five.

Isla giggled with delight. She'd never seen a cat high-five before. "Hiya, I'm Isla. What's your name?"

The cat meowed in response, then nudged its head against the cage door.

"Oh, you poor thing!" Isla cried. She tickled the cat's nose with her fingertips. Its rough, pink tongue licked at Isla's fingers as it purred contentedly.

Isla glanced at her watch – it was almost one o'clock. She'd promised Mum that she would leave at lunchtime to pack up her bedroom, ready for Gran's arrival. It had taken them ages to persuade Gran to come and stay for the summer and Isla wanted everything to be perfect. It was the first time Gran had visited since their beloved grandad had died in January. They all missed him so much and Isla knew what a big step it was for Gran. For ages, she'd hidden herself away, turning down invitations to visit, and refusing help of any kind. As the weeks had turned into months, it had felt like they'd lost Gran, too.

But last week, after lots of begging, Gran had finally agreed to come and stay. Isla couldn't wait to see her – Gran was almost as cat-crazy as she was, and didn't mind listening to Isla's constant ideas for persuading Mum to get a cat. The only downside was that it meant Isla had to share a room with her older sister Tilda, who wasn't at all keen on having a roommate.

"I have to go, but I'll come back later," Isla promised the cat, trying to tear herself away. It meowed loudly and she hesitated, glancing around to check that they were alone.

"OK!" she whispered. "You can come out

for a little while, just don't tell Mum. I'm not supposed to let the animals out – not after Basil. She thinks it could lead to some kind of disaster!"

A while ago, Isla had accidentally let a ferret escape, not knowing how fast a ferret can be. She had frantically chased it up and down the corridor for what felt like forever until she managed to coax it back into its cage with a piece of her ham sandwich. Unfortunately Mum had caught her in the act. She'd been so angry that Isla hadn't been allowed to come back to the vets for a week. Even Lucy – who never got mad with anyone – was ever-so-slightly cross with her.

Isla dropped her backpack, opened the cage and gently lifted up the cat, making sure she didn't hurt its bad leg. She hugged the cat so close that she could feel its heart beating, and rested her cheek on its soft fur, sighing happily.

"Your owner is the luckiest person in the world," Isla whispered. The cat meowed, batting at the air again with its front paw. Isla giggled, holding up her hand to meet it in another high-five. Down the corridor, Lucy's office door opened suddenly.

Isla hurriedly put the cat back into its cage, making triple sure that the door was secure, then leaned against the wall in what she hoped was an I'm-not-doing-anything-wrong kind of pose. Lucy and Mum stepped into the corridor, but they were so deep in conversation neither of them even noticed her.

"There's definitely no owner?" Mum asked.

"I'm afraid not," said Lucy. "There was no collar or identity chip, and we've had no reports of a missing cat. She was probably a stray in the wrong place at the wrong time when the car hit her. She might end up with a slight limp, but otherwise she'll make a full recovery. Hopefully someone will adopt her. She's such an affectionate cat."

Isla's eyes widened. A cat … *this* cat … needed a home! It couldn't be more perfect. How could she convince Mum though? Isla grabbed her notebook from her backpack, searching for her list again.

"Isla? What are you still doing here?" her mum called. "Shouldn't you be on your way home by now?"

"I was just coming to find you," Isla gabbled, hurrying over. Lucy gave her a smile. "I … um … couldn't help overhearing your conversation. I wasn't listening on purpose, I promise. I was just visiting the cat over there and I heard you say that she needs a home."

Isla's mum groaned. "Isla, honey, I've already told you—"

"I know, I know." Isla jumped in before Mum could say no again. She held up her notebook. "Just hear me out – I've got all these other ideas about why we should have a cat."

Her mum glanced at the notebook and gave a little smile. "I don't have time now,

Isla. We've got an emergency about to come in any second and you've got some packing to do – it's time you went home."

"But—"

"We'll talk about it later," Mum said.

"You promise you'll listen to me?" Isla asked.

Her mum nodded. Isla looked back sadly at the cat who had been watching them through the bars of the cage. It gave a small meow. "What's going to happen to her?"

"I'm taking her to the sanctuary tomorrow afternoon after we pick up your gran," Mum said. "Now off you go, and ask Tilda to make sure that Milo eats more than a packet of crisps for his lunch."

"I'll try," Isla said. "I'm not sure that she'll take any notice though." Isla was used to being ignored by her older sister.

Mum frowned. "Well, tell Tilda I'll be checking up on her later."

"I'll see you soon," Isla whispered to the cat as she left. Her mind was already buzzing with ideas. She was determined to convince Mum that the cat belonged with them. She couldn't bear the thought of her going to the sanctuary – not when they had a perfectly good home to give her. But Isla was going to need more than just a really good reason. She had to find the best reason *ever* ... and before tomorrow afternoon.

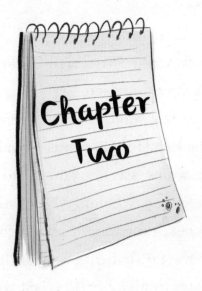

Chapter
Two

It was only a ten-minute walk home from
the vets. Isla ambled along the high street,
racking her brain for a way to persuade Mum
to change her mind about the cat. She passed
the small parade of shops – the bakery (which
made the best iced buns), the hairdressers, the
takeaway pizza place (where her family were
regular customers) and her favourite little
shop at the end, which sold everything from
biscuits to bubble bath – without glancing in

a single window. She was so deep in thought that she almost walked straight past the turning into her road.

Isla had already dismissed some of the ideas from her list, like how cats were so independent they practically looked after themselves. She was still considering reason number nine – that cats were brilliant hunters and could get rid of all the spiders in the house … probably. Isla wasn't sure about that one, but she thought Mum would like it. She always said that her love for small creatures didn't stretch as far as spiders. Isla sighed. Those ideas were good, but not really good. She needed perfect.

She let herself in and hurried upstairs. Tilda's door was shut but Isla could hear her sister on the phone inside. She opened the door a little and mimed eating at Tilda before pointing towards Milo's room. Tilda nodded and waved Isla away.

Milo was sitting on his bedroom floor engrossed in a comic, so Isla escaped into her bedroom to pack. An hour later, she crossed the last item off her *Things to Move to Tilda's Room* list and placed her notebook on top of the overflowing cardboard box. Her room seemed sadder somehow, without the mountain of cuddly toy cats piled on her bed and cute kitten posters on the walls. She tried to lift the box, but it wouldn't budge, so she leaned against it as hard as she could and shoved it through the doorway and on to the landing.

She shimmied in short bursts across the ancient green carpet and finally – ever so slightly out of breath – reached Tilda's bedroom. Isla knocked, but there was no reply, so she flung the door open to find Tilda sprawled across her bed clutching her phone.

Tilda was fifteen – four years older than Isla. It had never seemed like much of an age gap when they were younger, but now she barely spoke to Isla, preferring to hang out with her friends. Or her phone. Or her friends at the other end of the phone.

Tilda paused mid-text, catching sight of Isla's box. They both had the same oval-shaped faces, with a spattering of freckles and dark brown eyes, but apart from that the sisters were complete opposites. Isla loved animals and being outdoors, and Tilda loved… Isla wasn't actually sure what Tilda loved, apart from her phone and chocolate. She was hoping that Gran's visit might give them a chance for some sisterly bonding, although going by the look Tilda was giving her, Isla realized that was wishful thinking.

"What's all that?" Tilda demanded, her fingers tapping away wildly. Tilda could write and send a text in less than five seconds without even looking at the screen. Isla tried to pretend she wasn't impressed. "It's moving day, remember? Some help would be nice." Isla frowned. "You could have made some space for me – or tidied up."

My Stuff !! ← - ISLA

The single wardrobe in the corner looked like it had exploded, leaving a trail of brightly coloured skirts, jeans and tops scattered across the carpet. Tilda's bookshelves were stuffed with magazines and more colours of nail polish than Isla had thought existed and somewhere, camouflaged beneath the chaos, was a desk. That was another difference between the sisters. Isla liked to be neat and organized. Tilda liked everything in one place – the floor.

"There's plenty of room in the attic," Tilda replied with a sly grin.

Isla wrinkled her nose. "No way! It's dark and dusty and full of cobwebs."

To Isla's surprise, Tilda got up and started to drag the box towards a pull-out bed that Mum had found for Isla.

"Mum said that you could only bring the

essentials!" Tilda groaned, hauling the box through the clutter.

"It's *all* essential!" Isla insisted.

Tilda held up a cat-shaped money box. "This is not *essential.* There's barely enough space in here for me, let alone you *and* all your cat stuff!"

She snatched a cat cushion from the box, and threw it on to the landing. There was a button inside which made a noise when you pressed it, and the cushion landed on the carpet with a weak meow.

"And what are these?" Tilda dangled Isla's fluffy cat slippers in mid-air, her nose crinkling as though they had a nasty smell.

"Give them back!" Isla cried, rescuing the slippers. They were a size too small and her toes had almost made holes in the front, but she couldn't bear to part with them.

"Can I at least put up posters on my side of the room?" Isla asked. She had to admit that the room felt slightly cramped.

"One," Tilda said. "But no kittens."

"They're *all* kittens," Isla huffed. "And I've got seven."

"You do not need seven ca— Aaaaagh!" Tilda leaped on to the bed with an ear-piercing shriek, as a spider the size of her head scuttled across the floor.

Isla took one look and joined her sister on the bed. *This* was exactly why they needed a cat around the house. The spider stopped in the middle of the room, getting caught under a pair of pants. It spun in a circle wearing the polka-dot underwear like a hat. Isla leaned towards it cautiously. Aside from its gigantic size, something wasn't quite right with this spider. It made a strange whirring noise, and it moved in an awkward, robotic way. Stuck to one of its bristly legs was a note with "Gotcha!" scrawled across it in smudged felt tip. Isla passed the note to Tilda.

"Milo!" Tilda growled.

A mop of messy blond hair appeared as Milo peeked around the door, laughing, a remote control in one hand.

He tapped his ear, singing, "I can't hear youuuu!" then twisted the lever, making the spider do one last twirl before it scurried out of the room, the pants still on its head.

"I'm going to tell Mum you're not wearing your hearing aid!" Tilda yelled, as Milo fled to his room.

Isla winced. "You're not supposed to shout at him, remember?"

Milo could actually hear without his new hearing aid, but sometimes he found it difficult when lots of people were talking at the same time, or to make out quieter sounds. He was supposed to wear it every day over the summer to get used to it in time for the new school term, but he kept taking it off. Isla could kind of understand why he felt a bit self-conscious about wearing it, but she thought it was no different to her wearing glasses. She just wished Milo could see it that way.

Tilda returned to her phone and Isla opened her notebook to make a list of things to cheer Gran up, hoping for inspiration for cat ideas.

Ideas to Make Gran Happy Again
1. Baking

Gran loved baking. She had won first prize three years in a row at the Salford village fete for her Victoria sponge, but Mum said that Gran hadn't baked a thing since Grandad died. Not even one single shortbread biscuit, and they were Isla's favourite.

2. Zumba

Gran was not your average gran. It was what Isla loved most about her. She didn't sit around all day knitting tea cosies or doing whatever it was that other grans did. She went to a Zumba class on Monday nights, and hiked every weekend. She had two long walking poles that she insisted helped her walk faster. Isla thought she looked like she was trying to ski without snow.

3. Watch Funny Cat Videos

Isla scribbled this out and rewrote it at the top of the page. It was impossible to watch a cat doing a funny trick and not smile. She chewed the end of her pen, trying to think of something else that Gran might enjoy doing, when she noticed a pile of photographs on Tilda's bed.

"What are those?"

Tilda glanced up. "A few pictures Mum said I could have." She paused. "Of Grandad."

"Oh," Isla said quietly, a heavy feeling in her chest. It had been six months since Grandad died and not a day went by when she didn't miss him. "Can I see?"

Tilda scooped up the photos and nodded, giving Isla an awkward side-hug as she sat beside her. "He's so young in this one!"

Isla gave a sad sigh. She missed Grandad's smile so much. He'd been such fun. He'd have

Isla and Milo – and even Tilda – in stitches whenever they saw him.

"Is that Mum?" Isla pointed to a picture of her grandparents with a girl who looked about eleven – the same age as Isla.

Tilda handed Isla the photos. "Looks like it – she has Mum's super-thick hair." She grinned. "A bit like yours!"

Isla examined the photo. In it, Mum had a huge grin on her face as she cuddled a tiny black-and-white kitten.

"Do you think this was Mum's cat?" Isla wondered out loud. She flicked through the photos – the same cat was in almost every one.

Tilda shrugged. "Maybe. But that doesn't change things. Face it, Isla, Mum is *never* going to let you have a cat. Especially now Gran's coming to stay."

Isla waved her sister's words away.

Tilda grimaced. "I don't understand why you're so desperate for one anyway! They leave hair on everything and you have to change their smelly litter tray and remember to feed them all the time." She gestured to her phone. "You'd be better off getting a virtual cat. Less mess."

"You can't stroke a virtual cat though," Isla said. "And Gran loves cats as much as I do."

"True." Tilda laughed. "Remember that awful cardigan she wore last Christmas covered in cats wearing santa hats?"

Isla smiled, an idea sparking in her mind. Gran *did* love cats as much as she did. What if Gran's visit was actually the perfect time to get a cat?

Chapter Three

The next morning, Isla and her family
took the number fifteen bus to meet Gran
at the station. Despite her promise, Mum
had been too tired after work to listen
to anything Isla had to say about cats.
Isla had tried to ask about the cat in the
photographs over breakfast, but Mum was
flustered about being on time so Isla put
them in her backpack to show her later.

It had taken so long for Tilda to

straighten her hair and Milo to find his hearing aid (which Mum eventually located tucked inside a Wellington boot) that they missed the nine o'clock bus and had to wait in the pouring rain for the next one, listening to Tilda wail about the state of her hair. When it arrived, Milo insisted on sitting in his favourite spot at the front of the top deck. Isla sat with Mum in the row behind, doodling cats in her notebook to go with a story she'd written, while Tilda sat across the aisle, engrossed in her phone.

"I've been thinking about that gorgeous cat at Abbey Park with no home to go to," Isla said, abandoning her drawing because she couldn't get the cats' noses quite right.

"Surprise, surprise," Tilda muttered.

Mum gave Tilda a stern look and Tilda rolled her eyes, returning to her phone.

Mum had promised Isla her own phone for her twelfth birthday, but Isla was sure she wouldn't find it half as interesting as Tilda seemed to find hers.

"What happens if nobody adopts her?" continued Isla.

She had lain awake thinking about the cat all night. The sanctuary did their best, but it wasn't the same as being in a real home with people who loved you. Who looked after the cats at night? Who played with them or gave them hugs? The thought of that amazing cat going to the shelter was unbearable.

"Unfortunately it can be difficult homing an older cat," Mum admitted. "People prefer kittens because they're small and cute. She's a very pretty cat though," she added. "Smart, too. I'm sure someone will want her."

I want her, Isla thought. "She gave me a

high-five with her paw, and I'm sure she was talking to me."

Milo spun round. "A cat talked to you? What did it say – 'Meow are you?'"

Isla grinned. "That's purr-fect!"

Milo laughed and started waving at people on the street below. Most of the time they ignored him, but occasionally they'd wave or smile back and he'd wave even more.

"Tell Milo to stop!" Tilda hissed, sinking down in her seat. "He's so embarrassing."

"Sometimes your sister has a bad cat-titude," Mum said, winking at Isla.

Isla tried to smile, but she'd been working up the courage to ask something important, so the smile didn't quite make it to her face. She pulled the photographs out of her backpack. "I was wondering about these pictures…"

"Oh, look at my hair!" Mum laughed, when she saw the photos.

"Is the kitten yours?" Isla asked.

Mum nodded. "She was called Millie. She was my best friend … and so smart." Mum stared out of the window, lost in memories.

"Just like the cat at Abbey Park," said Isla. "She's super-smart, too. Couldn't … couldn't she live with us, Mum? Just for a little while? You're always saying how full they are at the cat sanctuary. You wouldn't have to do a thing, I promise – you would hardly even know she was there, and I've been thinking about Gran and how sad she's been since Grandad died, and…" Isla took a shaky breath. "Maybe having a cat around might cheer her up?"

"Oh, Isla, not this again! Having a pet is a big responsibility," Mum said gently. "Your gran isn't up to looking after an injured cat. It just isn't possible, especially now. We need to focus on helping Gran feel better."

Isla stared at the dirty floor. She was desperate to see Gran smile again. Having a cat around would be good for Gran – Isla was sure of it. She bit her lip to stop it wobbling.

"Can I say goodbye before you take her to the sanctuary?" she asked.

Mum patted Isla's hand. "I'm sure that would be OK."

Isla put the photos away and picked up her notebook, but she didn't feel like drawing any more.

Gran was already waiting at the station by the time they arrived. She still seemed like the same old Gran, with her lovely sweet cinnamon smell and her greying hair held off her face with a brightly coloured scarf. But her smile didn't look quite right – like when Tilda found out she wasn't invited to her friend's party and said she didn't care, but Isla could tell that wasn't true.

Isla gave Gran a big hug and insisted that she sit next to her on the bus home. As the bus crawled through the streets, she filled Gran in on all the pets she'd met at Abbey Park, and told her about helping out there during the holiday. The Gran of old would have been bursting with questions, but today she just listened as Isla told her about the snake who ate glasses and the cat with no tail.

By the time they made it back home, Mum was late for work.

"But it's Saturday!" Milo whined. "You said we could go to the park. I wanted to ride my bike."

"I know, honey," sighed Mum, ruffling Milo's hair. "But someone has to be there in case of an emergency. We'll go to the park tomorrow, I promise. Isla – you're in charge of settling Gran into her room. Is that OK, Mum?" She glanced at Gran who gave a little nod. "Tilda – make Gran a large cup of tea, and Milo –" Mum looked at Milo, hanging upside down on the sofa – "try to stay out of trouble."

"Don't forget about me saying goodbye to the cat later," Isla reminded her.

"Can I come?" Milo asked.

"I suppose so," Mum said, kissing them both on the head. "I'll call you in a bit."

Tilda put the kettle on, while Isla went upstairs with Gran to help her unpack, her mind still on the cat.

"Is something wrong, sweetheart?" Gran asked. "You're ever so quiet."

Isla put down the dress she was holding. "There's a cat at the vets who really needs a home. She's amazing, Gran! She's beautiful, and so smart. But ... Mum's taking her to the sanctuary today."

"Ah," Gran said. "You were hoping she could live here?"

Isla nodded and showed Gran the photographs of Mum and the kitten. "I thought these might remind her of how much she loved having a cat, but it didn't work."

Gran gave a small smile. "That's Millie.

She and your mum were inseparable – wherever one went, the other would follow. She was such a  lovely cat. But one day Millie went missing. We made posters and searched everywhere, but we never found her. Maybe your mum doesn't want you to go through the same pain she did when she lost Millie."

"That's so sad!" Isla sniffed. "Maybe that's why she won't let me have a cat."

Isla couldn't imagine how Mum must have felt losing Millie like that. No wonder she had never mentioned her.

"But this cat would be different!" Isla said. "Just because Millie went missing doesn't mean it will happen again."

Gran looked at the photo and sighed. "I'm afraid you have to do what your mum thinks is best, even if you don't agree with her."

It was nearly four o'clock when Mum phoned to say they could come up to Abbey Park. Isla raced to the front door shouting for everyone to get a move on. Tilda made a fuss, saying that she was old enough to stay at home by herself, but Gran told her that some fresh air would do them all good, so she reluctantly agreed. Milo couldn't stop bouncing with excitement the whole way there. He loved animals as much as Isla, but he was hardly ever allowed to visit Mum at work because he was a bit young.

Isla and Milo raced past Mum at the front

desk, ignoring her shouts to calm down. They dashed along the corridor and Isla let out a sigh of relief when she saw the cat holding its paw against the cage door.

"She remembers me!" Isla cried, as the cat gave a little meow and started purring.

Milo waved at the cat. "Meow are you?"

"Oh, Isla," Gran cried, as she, Tilda and Mum finally caught up. "You were right. She is a beautiful cat." The cat batted a paw in the air and Gran smiled. "Do you think I could give her a little hug?"

Mum opened the cage and carefully handed Gran the cat. Isla stood back and watched as Gran cooed and chatted to her happily. It had been so long since she'd seen Gran smile – really smile – that Isla couldn't quite believe it. She glanced up, catching Mum's eye – she'd noticed, too.

"Look how happy they are," she whispered to Mum. "They're a perfect match. *Please*, can she come home with us?"

Milo overheard and jumped up and down. "Oh, can she, can she?"

"It would be a shame if she couldn't find a proper home," Gran said, laughing as the cat meowed. "I think she thinks so, too!"

"Just say yes so that we can go home already," moaned Tilda, glancing up from her phone. "It smells like wet dog in here."

Mum watched Gran and the cat, her eyes shining, then blew out a long breath. "I'm probably going to regret this, but … if you're up for it, Mum … OK."

"Really?" Isla squealed, clapping her hands in excitement. Milo ran up and down the corridor whooping. Even Tilda gave a little smile.

Gran hugged the cat, giving her a kiss on her head. "I think we could become good friends."

"I have two conditions, however," Mum said. "One – I am not cleaning up after this cat when I've had a long day at work."

"You won't have to do a thing!" Isla promised.

"I'll help!" Milo added.

"Two – this is a temporary solution until we find her a more permanent home."

Isla nodded so hard she thought her head might fall off. "We can't keep calling her 'the cat', though."

"You should think of a name, Isla." Gran smiled. "After all, you're the reason she's found a home."

"*Temporary* home," Mum corrected.

Isla didn't need to think about it – she already had the perfect name. Ever since she'd fallen in love with cats, which was pretty much forever, she'd had a list of cat names. And at the very top of that list...

"Poppy," she said, beaming so much that her cheeks hurt. "Her name is Poppy."

Chapter four

That night, Isla found it impossible to sleep. She tossed and turned, her head full of ideas of things to do with Poppy and all the bits and pieces they would need to get for her arrival the next morning.

"Will you just go to sleep!" Tilda groaned beneath her duvet. "It's nearly midnight."

Isla sat up and switched on the small lamp next to her bed. "I can't! I'm too excited about Poppy coming home."

Isla had pleaded with Mum to let them take Poppy home immediately, but Mum said there was paperwork to fill out, and Lucy had to give Poppy a final check-up before she could be discharged. There was also the small issue of having absolutely nothing in the house for a cat.

Isla put her glasses on and reached under a pile of socks for Mum's old laptop.

"Now what are you doing?" Tilda asked.

"I have to tell Grace about Poppy!" Isla said. "She's going to be so jealous."

Her best friend Grace was on holiday in Cornwall, but she'd said she would check her emails on her mum's phone, "in case something mega-exciting happens while I'm away". Isla smiled to herself, imagining Grace's reaction when she read her email – this was definitely mega-exciting!

To: GraceMcNally
From: Islalovescats
RE: CAAAAAAAAAAAATSSSSS!!!!!

AMAZING NEWS!!! Remember the homeless cat at the vets I was telling you about? Well, Mum said we could bring her home with us! It's only temporary until she finds a forever home, but I am so excited! I named her Poppy and we're picking her up tomorrow after we've been shopping for cat things. I can't wait for you to meet her! She is so gorgeous and she's going to make Gran happy again!

Isla xx

PS – How is Cornwall? I miss you!

Isla clicked send and shut the laptop, then grabbed her notebook.

"There's so much to organize!" she said, making notes as she read through a *How to Look After Your Cat* leaflet. "I don't have time to sleep."

"Well, I do," Tilda grumbled, rubbing her eyes. "Just try to be quiet."

In ten hours Poppy would be theirs – *temporarily*, but still. There was no way Isla was going to be able to sleep. She wanted to make sure that they were totally prepared for Poppy's arrival. She already knew pretty much everything there was to know about looking after a cat, but she didn't want to make any mistakes or give Mum a reason to change her mind. Isla was determined to help Gran take such good care of Poppy that Mum wouldn't ever want to let her go.

In spite of having almost no sleep, Isla was up at seven o'clock, desperate for the day to begin. She pulled on the first clothes she could find and crept out of the bedroom. Tilda mumbled something about staying in bed because Isla had kept her awake all night and promptly went back to sleep. Isla bounced down the stairs and into the kitchen, grabbing Milo as he tried to dodge past her with a slice of toast. She spun him round until they fell in a heap on to the floor.

"I've been thinking," he mumbled after they'd both stopped laughing, "that we should call the cat Dynamo."

"Her *name* is Poppy."

Milo pouted. "Why do you get to name the cat?"

"Because she does," said Gran, coming into the kitchen. "Now, go and get dressed so we can visit the pet shop. Your mum had to go into work early so I'm in charge."

Milo looked down at the Spider-Man outfit he was wearing and grinned. "I *am* dressed."

Gran frowned. "Well, what about Tilda? Is she coming with us?"

"I don't think so," Isla said guiltily. "She didn't sleep very well last night."

It didn't take long to find everything they needed at the pet shop, thanks to Isla's list. They dropped all the stuff at home and then went straight to the vets to pick up Poppy.

"Now remember what we agreed," Mum

said, lifting Poppy into her new carrier. "This is temporary."

Isla tried to hide her grin, but she was so excited it was impossible. "I know. Just until we find Poppy a forever home."

She didn't add that she hoped Poppy's forever home was with them. For now, her dream had come true – they were finally getting a cat. Isla was so happy she thought she might burst.

"Can I carry her home?" Milo asked.

Mum and Gran exchanged looks. "I should probably carry her this time," Gran replied.

"I've checked her over and she looks fine," Lucy said. "She might be a bit nervous at first so give her plenty of space, and cuddles when she wants them, and don't let her outside on her own for a couple of weeks – just until she's used to the house."

"Promise me you won't get too attached?"
Mum said, looking at Gran, Isla and Milo.
"Any of you."

Isla nodded, crossing her fingers behind
her back. She didn't think she could make
such an impossible promise – she was
already head over heels in love with Poppy.

"Welcome home!" Isla said, as Gran set Poppy's carrier down on the floor. "Can we give her a tour?"

Mum had left strict instructions that Poppy was only allowed in the kitchen, conservatory and garden, but Isla thought it wouldn't do any harm to quickly show her the rest of the house. Besides, Poppy wouldn't be able to climb the stairs with her bad leg, anyway.

Gran nodded. "No loud noises though, Milo. She needs to settle in quietly."

"Come on, Poppy," Isla said, picking up the carrier. "I'll show you around."

Poppy gave a little meow of approval. They went up to Tilda's room first to let her know they were home, but it was empty.

"This is my room, too," Isla said. "Well, while Gran is here."

"Can we show her my room next?" Milo whispered.

Isla laughed. "You don't have to talk that quietly!"

Milo showed Poppy his entire comic collection and every single action figure he owned, and then Isla carried her downstairs.

"This is the sitting room," Milo said. "It's where we do most of our sitting!"

"There's a park across the road," Isla told Poppy, holding the carrier up to the big bay window. "Maybe we can take you when you're feeling better."

"I can push her on the swings!" Milo said.

"I don't think cats like swings," Isla giggled.

They wandered into the conservatory,

which ran along the back of the house and led out to the garden.

"This is where you'll be sleeping!" Isla said. She set the carrier down on the floor, lifted Poppy out and handed her to Gran.

Gran sat down on the small flowery sofa with Poppy purring happily on her lap, while Isla and Milo unpacked the bags from the pet shop. There was a bright pink cat bed, a scratching post with three levels that Gran had bought for when Poppy's leg was better, and two fish-shaped bowls – one for water and one for food. Mum said Poppy could go to the toilet in the garden via the cat flap that the previous owners had put in, but they'd also bought a litter tray just in case.

Isla had stuck one of her kitten posters on the wall and Milo had made a brightly

coloured banner decorated with paw prints,
which said *Welcome home, Dynamo!* Gran
set Poppy down on her new bed and Isla
fastened the purple collar she had bought
around Poppy's neck. It had a cute heart-
shaped tag engraved with Poppy's name
on one side and their phone number on
the other, so that she wouldn't get lost like
Millie had.

"You look right at home already, Poppy!" said Gran, smiling.

"Can I take her outside?" Isla asked.

"Just for a little while. Remember what Lucy said – Poppy needs to get used to us, and her new house."

Milo grabbed his scooter and zoomed outside on to the patio. Isla followed behind with Poppy. Mum never seemed to have time for the garden, so it was a bit overgrown, but perfect for a cat to explore.

They found Tilda lying on a blanket spread out in the sun, listening to music through her headphones.

"That's Tilda," Isla told Poppy. "She's always on her phone so she probably won't notice you."

Tilda looked up and rolled her eyes. Isla was about to put Poppy down when a ball flew over the fence, narrowly missing Isla's head. She squealed, squeezing Poppy a bit too tightly. Poppy dug her claws into Isla's arm making her squeal even more.

A moment later, Sam, her next door neighbour, popped his head over the fence.

"Sorry! Can I have my ball back?"

"You almost hit me!" Isla snapped. "And Poppy. I could have dropped her!"

"I didn't mean to," he muttered. Sam had been in Isla's class at school. They were sort of friends, but some days she liked him more than others.

"You got a cat?" Sam asked.

Isla put Poppy down on the grass. "She's my gran's cat really, but while she's here she belongs to all of us. She's not just any cat either," Isla said proudly. "Watch."

She held her hand up to Poppy who tapped it with her paw.

"Cool!" Sam gasped. "Can she do any other tricks?"

"Well, she's got a poorly leg so I'm not sure she can do tricks, but she can talk … kind of," Isla said. "Say hello to Sam, Poppy."

Poppy gave a little meow and Sam laughed. "Wow! Maybe you could teach her some other stuff?" Sam suggested. "I could help."

Before Isla could answer, Tilda ran over, waving her phone in Poppy's face. Poppy swatted at the phone with her paw and

Tilda laughed. "That's brilliant! Make her wave again, Isla."

"You can't just *make* her do it," Isla huffed.

Poppy batted at the air again. Tilda videoed it and looked back at Isla smugly. "Perfect!" she squealed and disappeared into the house.

Perfect for what? Isla frowned, wondering what Tilda was up to. She threw the football back to Sam and scooped up Poppy.

"Let me know when her leg's better," Sam said, disappearing behind the fence.

"I will," Isla replied. She went back inside to find Mum chatting away to Gran in the kitchen. "What are you doing home?"

"It was a bit quiet at the vets so Lucy said I could come home early," Mum explained.

Isla paused. "To check up on us?"

"No, Isla," Mum said, reaching out to

♡ 66 ♡

stroke Poppy's ears. "To see how Poppy was getting on."

Milo came into the kitchen clutching his stomach. "I'm so hungry! Will you make us some chocolate brownies, Gran?"

"Maybe I can bake you something?" Mum offered.

Milo and Isla looked at each other and burst out laughing.

"What?" grumbled Mum. "It's not that ridiculous. I could bake something if I wanted to."

"You *could*," Isla said. "I'm just not sure that you *should*."

The last time Mum had baked, she'd made cookies for the school fair but forgotten they were in the oven. There had been so much smoke that the neighbours had called the fire brigade. Luckily there hadn't been an actual fire, but it had taken weeks to get rid of the horrible smell.

"We don't want to burn the house down, do we?" chuckled Gran. "But I'm afraid I can't bake something for you, Milo."

"You can't?" Milo said, disappointed.

"No, but I *can* teach you how to bake. There really should be at least one person in this house who knows how to make cookies. Maybe we could bake a cake for Poppy as a welcome to the family?"

Isla held her breath, waiting for Mum to say the word *temporary* again, but she just smiled.

Chapter
Five

"Do I *have* to come to the vets today?"
Isla asked Mum on Monday morning. She
had had such a brilliant weekend playing
with Poppy while Gran and Milo baked
everything from chocolate-chip cookies to
bread rolls, she didn't want it to end.

"You usually love coming to the vets
with me," Mum said, surprised.

"I do! But I was planning to invite Grace
and Ayesha over to meet Poppy."

"Well, they can't come today, I'm afraid. Tilda's going over to Misha's, and Gran's taking Milo to a karate competition. I really don't want you at home by yourself all day."

"I won't be by myself," Isla said, scooping Poppy into her arms. "Poppy's here."

"Nice try!" Mum smiled. "You'll get plenty of time to play with Poppy later. Why don't you see if Grace and Ayesha want to come for a sleepover tomorrow?"

Isla put Poppy down and raced upstairs to email her friends – a sleepover with Poppy would be brilliant! There was an email from Ayesha saying she couldn't wait to tell Isla about her trip to Japan and meet Poppy, and a reply from Grace to Isla's email which basically said *OMG!!!* over and over again. Isla sent them both a quick message inviting them over the next day.

"How is Perry doing?" Isla asked one of their regular visitors – Mrs Meadows who was there with her son, Tyler.

"Sausages," Perry squawked.

"He's fine," Mrs Meadows said with a sigh, holding up the cage so that Isla could see the colourful parrot inside. "Just here for a check-up."

"Mushy peas," Perry squawked at Isla.

Isla giggled. "Why's he saying that?"

"*Somebody*," Mrs Meadows said, glancing sideways at Tyler, "thought it would be funny to teach Perry some new words. Now he won't say anything but types of food."

"Cheese and crackers," Perry squawked, bobbing his head up and down.

Lucy called Perry through to the

treatment room. There were no more patients waiting to be seen, so Isla sat behind the front desk, working on a picture of Poppy she'd planned to surprise Gran with. Usually a lady called Susan worked on reception, but she'd called in sick with a cold so Mum was frantically going back and forth between the front desk and the treatment rooms.

The bell over the front door chimed, startling Isla as a man hurried in holding a cat carrier.

"Can I help you?" Isla asked in her politest voice.

"I need to talk to someone about this cat."

"Is it hurt?" Isla asked.

The man shook his head. "Is there anyone else I can speak with? An adult, maybe?"

Isla was about to say that actually, even though she was eleven, she knew everything

♡ 72 ♡

there was to know about cats, when Mum
rushed in with a handful of files.

"Has Mr Smith arrived with his bulldog
yet?" she puffed, dropping the files on the
desk. She looked up, noticing the man and
the cat carrier.

"Is everything OK?" Mum asked, coming
round in front of the desk. "Can I help?"

She and the man had a whispered
conversation, gesturing at the cat carrier
every so often. Isla kneeled down and peered
in through the door. A gorgeous
fluffy grey cat with icy blue
eyes stared back at her.
He was small – not quite
a kitten, but not a fully
grown cat either. Isla
guessed he was maybe
six months old.

"If he's not unwell or injured then you're going to have to take him to the cat sanctuary," Mum said, narrowing her eyes at the man in the same way she sometimes did at Milo when he'd done something she wasn't too pleased about. "I'll give them a call to see if they have any space. I'm sure the number's here somewhere." She shuffled through some papers on the desk, then threw her hands up in despair.

"Can you just hold on while I find the number?" Mum said, already halfway out the room.

The man paced up and down, while Isla peeked in at the little cat again. She wanted to ask why he was abandoning a perfectly good cat, but she didn't want to get in trouble. She forced herself to stay quiet even though she didn't really understand.

She squinted at the cat's collar, which had a silver tag engraved with the name "Roo".

"Hi, Roo," she cooed, poking her finger in and out through the cat carrier's door in a little game as Roo swiped at it.

"The sanctuary's full, I'm afraid," Mum said, reappearing. "You'll have to—" She paused. "Where did he go?"

Isla looked up, frowning. The waiting room was empty. "He was here a minute ago."

Mum ran to the door, but the man had vanished.

"Why did he do that?" Isla asked shakily. "Why would he leave Roo behind?"

"I don't know, honey." Mum sighed, looking down at Roo. "He said he'd bought the cat as a birthday present for his daughter. Unfortunately, they're moving to a rented house where they're not allowed animals."

"It's so sad," whispered Isla, taking Roo out of the carrier. "Look at him, he's so small. Maybe we can make the man change his mind?"

She turned over the name tag for a clue about who the man was or where he lived, but it was blank. Isla hoped the man's daughter wouldn't be too upset.

Mum opened her mouth as though she was about to say something, then firmly shut it again, pressing the buzzer to call Lucy to the front desk. Isla hugged Roo closer. If the cat sanctuary was full, where was he going to go?

Lucy appeared a few minutes later with a happier-looking Mrs Meadows. Isla said goodbye to Tyler and Perry, who called out "Sausages!" again as they left.

"I *would* take the cat," said Lucy after Mum had explained what had happened. "But I've got a full house as is it with the new puppy. Maybe you could...?"

Mum's shoulders drooped. Isla gasped out loud, realizing what Lucy was saying.

"Oh! We could take him, couldn't we? He's so tiny he'll hardly take up any space. And he'd be company for Poppy."

Mum looked at Lucy, who gave a little smile.

"What have I started?" Mum groaned. "All right! But *only* until the cat sanctuary has room for him. Our house is not Palmer's Home for Lost and Lonely Cats."

Isla whooped with joy, thinking that actually it would be quite brilliant if their house was *just* that. She spun Roo in a victory twirl and laughed. She couldn't

quite believe it, but they'd gone from
having no cats to having two … and if she
had anything to do with it, she was going
to make sure that neither of them ever left.

"What's for dinner?" Isla asked on the way home, trying not to swing a sleeping Roo too much inside the cat carrier.

"I'm too exhausted to cook anything." Mum yawned. "I'll order pizza."

"We had pizza yesterday," Isla laughed.

"Pasta it is then."

Sam was playing football with his friends in the park as they passed by. Isla waved to get his attention, pointing at the cat carrier. She was sure that he glanced her way, but one of the other boys followed his gaze and laughed at him, and he quickly turned back to the game.

"He probably didn't see you," Mum said, opening their front door as Isla frowned.

"What have you got there?" Milo asked,

bounding to meet them in the hallway.

Isla grinned. "Another cat! He's called Roo and he's coming to live with us."

"*Temporarily!*" Mum shouted from the doorway.

"Look, Milo! He's so cute," said Isla.

Gran and Poppy came to see what all the fuss was about. "How did you manage to persuade your mum to take in another cat?" Gran asked with a wink.

"I didn't have much choice!" Mum said.

Poppy put a paw up to the carrier and meowed. Roo meowed in return.

"Oh, they love each other already!" Isla gasped.

"Don't get any ideas, Isla," Mum warned. "Let's put Roo in the conservatory and give him some space to settle in." She looked round. "What's that delicious smell?"

"Dinner," Gran replied. "Come on, it's getting cold."

They followed Gran to the kitchen to find Tilda looking ravenous. In the middle of the table was a shepherd's pie, carrots, peas and a huge jug filled to the brim with steaming gravy. Isla didn't know who was more shocked – her or Mum.

"Thank goodness you're home," said Tilda, eyeing the pie. "Gran said we couldn't start until everyone was here."

"I thought we could do with a nice home-made meal." Gran smiled.

Chapter Six

"Look at this," Tilda said, as Isla wandered into the kitchen the next day. Tilda spun the laptop round on the table, showing Isla a YouTube video.

"Oh! It's Poppy." Isla watched as Poppy meowed and waved at the screen. "Is that what you filmed in the garden? She's so cute."

"Never mind that." Tilda pointed to the bottom of the screen. "Look at how many people have watched the video. Nearly two hundred already! We're going to have to make some more videos – of Roo, too."

"Why?"

Tilda huffed. *"Because* the more videos you have, the more people will watch them, and Poppy will be famous."

Isla didn't think Poppy cared whether she was famous or not, but at least Tilda seemed happy to have the cats around. She would need Tilda on her side if she was going to convince Mum to let them stay forever.

There was a knock at the front door and Isla hurried to open it. She found Grace and Ayesha chatting excitedly on the doorstep, weighed down by sleeping bags and pillows.

"I can't believe your mum finally let you have a cat!" Grace squealed, hugging Isla. They had only been apart for a week or so, but to Isla it felt like a lifetime. She led her friends into the lounge so they could offload their things.

"Two cats!" Isla grinned, picking up Roo as he tried to sneak outside. "Meet Roo!"

Grace and Ayesha gasped in surprise as Isla told them all about the man at the vets and how Mum had had no choice but to let Roo come home with them.

"You are *so* cute!" Grace said, stroking Roo's head. "And you are so lucky, Isla! I told my mum about Poppy and how it's so unfair that you get to have a cat when I don't, but she said we can't have any pets because Dad is allergic to animals. I don't think he is really though, because last year in Egypt he rode on a camel and was totally fine. I think he's just allergic to the *idea* of getting a pet. Every time I try to talk to him about it he gets all red and blotchy."

Isla and Ayesha laughed. Isla had really missed them. They'd been friends since nursery, when they'd all worn the same *Hello Kitty* dress one day, and had been inseparable ever since. When they were younger, they'd worn matching outfits, pretending to be triplets even though they looked nothing like each other and Ayesha had always been quite a bit shorter than Grace and Isla.

"Come on," Isla said, cuddling Roo and heading for the conservatory. "I'll introduce you to Poppy."

Poppy was sitting in her bed, looking as if she'd been waiting for them.

"Oh, she's adorable," cried Grace. She sat down next to Poppy, who immediately held up her paw to say hello.

"You are so, so lucky, Isla," said Ayesha. "If Poppy and Roo lived at my house, I'd never want to go out again!"

Isla smiled. She knew exactly how Ayesha felt.

They played with Poppy and Roo for a while, and then headed into the kitchen in search of Gran's chocolate fudge cake.

"Shall we go to the park after this?"

Grace suggested, as she helped herself to a second slice.

Isla hesitated. She wasn't sure that she wanted to run into Sam and his friends again. She told Grace and Ayesha about how he'd ignored her last time and they nodded sympathetically.

"Boys!" Grace said.

"My brother's exactly the same," Ayesha said. "Whenever we're out somewhere and he sees anyone he knows from school, he acts like he doesn't know me!"

"At least you won't see Sam at school any more," said Grace.

Isla and Grace and a few of their friends from primary school were starting at Langford High in a few weeks' time. Sam was going to a posh boys' school in the city.

Isla grimaced. "I wish you hadn't

mentioned school," she said. "I'm not sure I'm ready for Langford High – it's so huge. What if I get lost trying to find the science lab or something?"

Tilda had told her about a Year 7 girl who had got on the wrong bus and ended up having to walk five miles back home.

"At least you'll have Grace," Ayesha said. "I don't know anyone going to my new school. What if nobody likes me?"

"Of course they'll like you," Isla said, giving her a hug. "And you'll always have us."

"Definitely," Grace nodded, jumping down from the table. "Come on, let's go."

"We're going to the park, Gran," Isla shouted. She could hear Gran chatting away to Poppy in the conservatory and wondered if she might be lonely without her own friends close by.

"Don't be too long," Gran called back. "Your mum is getting Chinese for dinner on her way home from work."

As they headed over to the park, Isla saw her neighbour Mr Evans cutting the hedge in his front garden. He was about the same age as Gran and lived on his own, too. Isla stopped suddenly. What if Mr Evans was a bit lonely as well…?

"I've just had the best idea!" Isla said. She explained her plan to her friends.

"I'm not sure about this," said Grace, glancing over at Mr Evans. "What if he doesn't want a new friend?"

"Do they have anything in common?" asked Ayesha.

Isla paused for a moment, frowning. "Well, they both like tea," she said as Mr Evans took a sip from his mug.

Grace rolled her eyes. "What if that's coffee?"

"Is everything OK, girls?" Mr Evans called.

Isla nodded. "I was wondering if you might want to come over – to meet my gran," she said hurriedly. "I mean … my gran has come to stay with us for a little while and she wanted me to ask you if you'd like to come over for a … cup of tea?"

"Isla!" Ayesha squeaked under her breath as Grace giggled.

"Never mind," Isla said. "I'm sorry to have bothered you."

"I'd love to," Mr Evans said. "That's very kind of her to invite me." He gestured to the hedge. "I'll have to finish this first, but tell your gran I'll be over in half an hour."

"Perfect!" Isla grinned, linking one arm

with Grace and the other with Ayesha.

"I don't think you should have done that," Ayesha said as they hurried off. "Now he thinks your gran invited him."

"It'll be fine," Isla said, feeling a little less confident than she sounded. "I just need to explain everything to Gran before he arrives."

The park was empty and there was no sign of Sam and his friends. They swung on the swings for a while, chatting more about how weird boys could be and what their new school uniforms looked like, until Isla noticed the time.

"We'd better get back," she said, "or Mr Evans will be there before us."

There was no sign of their neighbour as they headed into the kitchen. Isla breathed a small sigh of relief. But she still had to explain things to Gran, and now they were here, she didn't quite know what to say to her.

Grace nudged her under the table. "You should tell her," she whispered.

"What are you whispering about?" Gran asked, eyeing them suspiciously.

"Nothing," Isla mumbled, stuffing more chocolate cake into her mouth. Maybe Mr Evans had had second thoughts... She really hoped so.

Just then there was a knock at the door. Gran went to answer it, and they could hear muffled voices in the hallway. Isla didn't know if it was because of all the cake she'd eaten, but she suddenly felt quite sick.

Poppy jumped up on to Isla's lap and meowed, batting a paw towards the hallway.

"I think Poppy wants you to go and explain," said Ayesha.

Isla carried Poppy
to the front door
where Gran and
Mr Evans gave Isla
a look that said she
was in a little bit of
trouble.

"Hi, Mr Evans,"
she said weakly.

"Isla," Gran said.
"Mr Evans said that
you invited him over?"

Isla bit her lip and nodded, not daring
to look at Mr Evan's face to see how angry
he was.

"You said your gran was the one who
invited me?" he asked, puzzled.

"I just thought you both might like some
company. I was worried you were getting a

bit lonely," she said to Gran.

Gran laughed. "Honestly, Isla! You could have told me. How could I possibly be lonely? I have all of you to keep me company, and Poppy."

"You're not cross?"

"Well, I don't really need you to find friends for me, and I'm sure neither does Mr Evans –" she gave him an apologetic smile – "but I know you only had my best interests at heart, so no, I'm not cross."

Poppy waved her paw at Mr Evans. He laughed and said, "Hello to you, too!"

Gran invited him in and told him all about Poppy. Before Isla knew it, they were chatting away as though they were old friends, over a cup of tea and cake.

"See," said Isla to Grace and Ayesha. "I told you they both liked tea."

"Where are we going to sleep?" Ayesha asked after they had polished off the last of the Chinese.

Isla frowned. Usually they all slept in her bedroom, but they couldn't now that Gran was here, and there was no way they would all fit in Tilda's room.

"I've got an idea!" she said, as Poppy wandered past, closely followed by Roo. "Wait here a moment." Isla ran upstairs and grabbed as many cushions and blankets as she could carry.

When she returned, Ayesha and Grace followed Isla into the conservatory where Roo and Poppy had settled into their cat beds for the night. They watched Isla curiously as she spread out the blankets and cushions on the floor.

"Perfect!" Grace cried.

"It's almost like camping out under the stars," said Ayesha.

Isla grinned. "And best of all, we get to snuggle with these two!"

They changed into their pyjamas and Isla wriggled into her sleeping bag beside her friends. Ayesha had a kimono-style dressing gown covered with a beautiful cat design.

Isla gasped. "I haven't asked you about Japan!" she said to Ayesha, a guilty flush spreading across her face. She'd been so wrapped up in the cats, not to mention Gran and Mr Evans, and her worries about Sam and school that she'd completely forgotten about Ayesha's trip. "Tell me everything!"

"It was a-mazing!" said Ayesha.

She pulled out some photographs that she'd brought with her. There were so many people and so many brilliant things that Ayesha had taken pictures of, including a toy shop which had loads of really cool-looking toys, and a beautiful temple with a roof made from bamboo.

"We stayed with my grandparents in their apartment in Shinjuku – that's in Tokyo – and one day they took us here." Ayesha showed Isla the next photograph. "You'll love this one, Isla."

"A café?" Isla asked.

"Not just any café," Ayesha said, handing her some more photographs. "Take a closer look."

Isla gasped. At first it seemed like any other café with people sitting eating cake, and drinking cups of tea, but then she noticed that they were surrounded by cats. Some were asleep in cat beds, others were on people's laps enjoying a lot of fuss and attention. On the floor, a cat batted a ball of wool between its paws, whilst another attempted to climb a scratching post.

"It's a cat café," Ayesha explained.
"They're huge in Japan. They're perfect for people who love cats but can't have one of their own. Like me!" Ayesha grinned.

"It's brilliant!" Isla breathed. She was definitely going to add Japan to her *Places to Visit* list in her notebook.

There was a sudden movement behind the sofa and Isla held a finger to her lips, leaning to peer over the top. "Milo!" she cried. "What are you doing back there?"

"I … um … lost something," he said sheepishly, bobbing up to wave at Grace and Ayesha.

"You were eavesdropping more like!" Isla said, ushering him out of the conservatory. "You should be in bed!"

Milo ran off giggling and Isla snuggled back into her sleeping bag. Roo jumped out of his bed and climbed over Isla's legs, nuzzling at her hand. She scooped him up with a sigh, snuggling her face into his fur as he settled down to sleep beside her.

"Do you think Sam was ignoring me because he was embarrassed?" Isla said quietly.

Grace yawned and stroked Poppy, who had curled up on the end of her sleeping bag. "I'm sure it was just because he was with his friends."

"He was probably too engrossed in playing football," Ayesha added.

If only people were as easy to understand as cats, Isla thought.

Chapter Seven

Isla spent the rest of the week with Poppy
and Roo in the garden. The weather was
gloriously sunny and she and Milo had been
slowly introducing Roo and Poppy to the
outside world, and each other. Luckily Poppy
was an easy-going cat, so she didn't seem to
mind when Roo batted at her tail with his
paw or tried to pounce on her playfully. Milo
loved Poppy, but she was with Gran most
of the time. Roo, however, was a cat version

of Milo – with matching energy levels. They spent so much time running about and rolling around the garden that Isla felt exhausted just watching them.

By the time Saturday arrived, everyone was looking forward to a quiet weekend. As they were enjoying a lazy breakfast, the phone rang. Mum went to answer it leaving everyone to fight over the last croissant.

"Exciting news!" Mum sang, hanging up a few minutes later. "That was Lucy. The *Abbey Park Chronicle* is going to write an article about the vets and they want to interview us!"

"Brilliant!" Isla said, buttering a slice of toast. "Lucy does such great work – you too, Mum—"

"Wait," interrupted Tilda. "You said they want to interview *us?*"

"Yes!" said Mum. "All of us. It's a bit short notice, but they're coming to the house today. Lucy said they want some photographs of Poppy and Roo as well, because they both came from the vets, and they're also planning to write about the local cat sanctuary and the need to find the cats new homes."

"But they can't!" Isla cried. "What happens if someone sees Roo or Poppy in the newspaper and decides they want to adopt them?"

Tilda frowned at Isla. "I think that might be the point."

Milo looked up from his comic. "But … Roo's my sidekick! He can't leave."

Isla felt tears prick her eyes. She couldn't bear to lose the cats now that she'd finally got them. "They're so used to us, though. They think this is their home – it *is* their home."

Gran, who had been sitting quietly with Poppy on her lap, spoke up. "I've been thinking about that, actually. I've grown rather fond of Poppy, and I've decided that – if it's all right with everybody – I'd like to keep her."

Isla gave Gran a wobbly smile. She'd been hoping Gran would say say that. Wherever Gran went, Poppy was never far behind. It was clear how much they loved each other. All she needed now was for Mum to let them keep Roo.

Mum smiled. "What does everybody else think?"

Tilda shrugged. "Fine by me."

"Milo?" Gran asked.

Milo screwed up his face tightly, as though he was thinking really hard about it. "Ummmmm. We can still give Poppy hugs all the time, right?"

Gran laughed. "Whenever you want."

Milo gave her a thumbs up.

Gran looked at Isla. "Isla?"

"It won't really change anything, will it?" Isla sniffed. "You'll both still be here with us. I just wish we could keep Roo, too."

"And me," said Milo glumly.

Gran and Mum exchanged a look. "Isla, honey. I'm not trying to find a new home for Roo," said Mum. "Lucy and I just thought the article might be a good way to get people's attention. Think of all the other homeless cats out there."

Isla's breath caught in her throat.

"Does that mean we can keep him?"

Mum gave her a hug. "As long as you promise to keep a better eye on him. I found him curled up in the bottom of my wardrobe this morning."

Isla nodded. "You're not going to change your mind and take him to the cat sanctuary?"

"I can't believe I'm saying this, but no – Roo can stay. But he's *your* responsibility, so you need to make sure you look after him properly."

"Oh! I will, I promise!" Isla grabbed Roo and hugged him tightly, crying happy tears this time. "You're mine, Roo! You're really mine!" Roo gave a little meow, wriggling to get free. Isla set him back down and he scurried over to Gran and Poppy.

"He's mine, too!" Milo pouted.

"Of course he is," said Mum, handing Isla a tissue. "And we need to make sure both Poppy and Roo are looking their best for the newspaper. So I suggest you fetch their brush, Isla, and get to work."

"I'm going to be famous!" Tilda squealed as she tapped away at her phone to tell her friends.

"The *cats* are going to be famous," corrected Isla.

"Well, yes – especially Poppy when they see how clever she is – but she'll need a human representative. She can't go to interviews by herself or do television adverts and things like that."

"Cats do television adverts," Milo piped up. "You see them all the time."

Tilda ignored him. "What time are the people from the *Chronicle* coming?"

There was a knock at the door and Tilda jumped.

"Oh!" said Mum, glancing at her watch. "That can't be them already?"

"Someone stall them!" Tilda called as she bolted up the stairs. "I need to find the perfect outfit."

Milo's eyes went wide and he ran after her. Gran quickly cleared the table while Isla sorted out the cats. She grabbed the cat brush, and ushered Poppy and Roo into the conservatory, grooming them until their coats were so silky-looking, they shone.

"Best behaviour, please," Isla said to Roo as he tried to chew the end of the brush. She pulled it out of his reach and gave Poppy a hug. "Show them how amazing you are."

♡ 108 ♡

Having the newspaper people over wasn't half as interesting as Isla thought it would be. There was lots of standing around doing nothing while they waited for the photographer to arrive. Then they'd had to rearrange the garden furniture for the photos because the light was better in the garden. The reporter was a woman called Sally Smithers who was only really interested in talking to Mum, as she worked at the vets.

Tilda followed Sally around like a shadow, nodding at everything she said and interrupting whenever she asked a question.

Isla watched Dan the photographer as he set up his camera and other equipment. There was a big white umbrella to reflect light on to whoever he was photographing, and a huge, floppy silver disk that had the same effect.

Tilda made her way over, clearly bored with trying to get Sally's attention. "Do you want to take some pictures of me?" she asked Dan, giving him her best smile.

Dan nodded politely. "I'm sure Sally will want some family shots, but first I need to take some pictures of your mum. Would you mind holding this for me?" He handed Tilda the disk.

Isla smiled to herself as Tilda held up the disk while Dan snapped away at Mum with Poppy and Roo.

When the interviews were over, Mum offered everyone a cup of tea and a slice of Gran's chocolate cake. Poppy rubbed against Sally Smithers's legs for attention.

"What a friendly cat you are, Poppy," said Sally, stroking the top of Poppy's head. "I can see why the Palmers wanted to keep you!"

Poppy meowed and held up her paw to bat at Sally's hand. Sally almost choked on her cake. "She gave me a high-five, Dan!" she cried. "You must get a picture of this."

Dan hurried over, with Tilda hot on his heels.

"Why don't you take a family shot?" said Sally. "With Poppy high-fiving one of the children!"

As the family gathered together, Isla looked round for Milo. He still hadn't come down from his room.

"Hang on, we're missing Milo," she called, hurrying indoors. "I'll go and find him."

Poppy ignored everyone's calls for her to stay still and followed Isla indoors. They eventually found Milo inside his wardrobe with one of his favourite superhero comics.

"Are you coming downstairs?" Isla asked.

Milo stroked Poppy as she climbed on to his lap. "I've decided I don't like having my photo taken."

"Because of this?" Isla asked gently, pointing to his hearing aid.

Milo nodded.

"Look at Poppy," Isla said. "She's got a limp, but nobody cares."

"She's a cat," Milo mumbled. "People don't laugh at cats."

"They're not going to laugh at you

either, Milo," Isla said. "I wear glasses to help me see, and Tilda had to have braces to make her teeth straight. Your hearing aid is just like that – it helps you to hear."

She pointed at his comic. "Anyway, how are you going to be a superhero and save the day if you don't wear your hearing aid? You won't be able to hear anyone calling for help!"

Milo giggled. "I'm glad Poppy and Roo don't have to leave," he said, snuggling into Poppy who purred happily.

"Me, too." Isla smiled. "Come on, let's go and help Poppy and Tilda have their starring moment."

Chapter Eight

Tilda checked the *Chronicle* every day
that week, hoping to see her picture in
the paper. By Saturday, the article still
hadn't come out and everyone was feeling
disappointed after the excitement of being
interviewed. Gran decided they should have
a Sunday roast to cheer themselves up.

She popped the meat in the oven and
went upstairs to find her glasses, leaving
Isla and Mum peeling vegetables – it was

the only thing she trusted them to do.

Tilda was sitting at the kitchen table, working away on the laptop. She said she had homework to do over the summer, but every time Isla came near she pulled the laptop away secretively.

Milo bounded into the kitchen clutching a shoebox with holes poked into the sides.

"Do you want to see my pet mouse?" he asked Tilda, holding the box out.

"I'm not falling for that one again," said Tilda, staring at the screen.

"It's not a toy!" Milo insisted. "It's a real live mouse." He peeped into the box and frowned. "Well, I think it's live. It was moving when Roo gave it to me, but it's asleep now."

Isla glanced at Roo, who was looking very pleased with himself. "Mum, I think

you'd better take a look at Milo's mouse.
I think it might be … ill."

Mum looked up in alarm. "Milo, honey,
where did you get the mouse from exactly?"

Milo prodded at the small brown lump
inside the box. It didn't move.

"Nobody ever listens to me!" he huffed.
"I told you – Roo gave it to me."

"It's a real mouse?" Tilda squealed.

Mum reached for the box, but Milo
pulled it away. He placed the box on the
table and lifted the mouse out.

"Let me have a little look, Milo," said
Mum gently. "I just want to make sure
the mouse is OK. I'm an animal nurse,
remember?"

As Milo slowly lifted his hand towards
Mum, Isla feared the worst for the poor
creature, but as Mum leaned down to take a

closer look, the mouse jumped out of Milo's hand and landed at Tilda's feet.

Tilda screamed as it scurried over her bare toes and climbed on to the kitchen table. Roo took off after the mouse as it raced down the hallway heading for the stairs, with Poppy limping after them.

"My mouse!" Milo wailed, chasing after them.

"Grab the box," Mum told Isla. "We need to get it out of the house before Gran sees it. She's terrified of mice!"

"Too late," Isla grimaced, as a loud shriek came from upstairs.

"*She's* terrified of mice!" Tilda squeaked. "It touched *me*! It actually touched *me* with its tiny claws."

Isla hurried upstairs after Mum. They found Gran sitting on her bed hugging her knees as the cats pawed beneath the bed.

"This is exactly why I didn't want cats in the house!" Mum yelled, as she tried to catch hold of Roo.

"You can't blame Roo!" Isla said defensively. "He was only doing what cats are supposed to do. Here, let me help."

Isla kneeled down and reached slowly under the bed until she felt a tiny quivering furball. She scooped up the terrified mouse, holding tight enough that it couldn't escape, but not so tight that she might accidentally squash it. Milo hugged her as she placed the mouse back into the box.

Gran breathed a sigh of relief. "What a fright that gave me. I think I could do with a strong cup of tea!"

That afternoon, after a stomach-bursting roast lunch, Gran and Milo took over the kitchen.

"What's going on?" asked Mum. "Aren't you full from lunch?"

"Mr Evans is coming over," said Milo, as he tried to mix a bowlful of thick cake mixture.

Mum raised her eyebrows at Gran.

"He's coming for afternoon tea with some of his friends," Gran explained. "To meet Poppy."

Isla looked up from the picture of Roo she'd been sketching and gave Gran a little smile. Gran seemed so much like her old self again. There were still times when Isla saw her looking sad, but she was sure that Gran was feeling a lot better. She was baking almost every day with Milo, and their house had never been so tidy and organized. Not to mention Gran's amazing home-cooked meals. It had been ages since they'd had a sniff of a takeaway.

Roo ran out into the garden and Isla followed him with her notebook and pencil, determined to get him picture perfect.

"Hi, Isla," Sam called, appearing over the fence.

"Oh, you're talking to me again now, are you?" Isla replied stiffly. "Is that because your friends aren't around?" She was still cross at the way he'd ignored her, though secretly she was glad to see him.

Sam's cheeks reddened. "I'm sorry," he blurted out. "I was going to come over – honest – but by the time I turned round you were gone. I guessed you might be mad at me about it, so I've been waiting until you were a bit less mad."

"Huh!" Isla huffed, giving him a small smile.

Sam gave her a relieved-looking smile in return.

"I saw you in the newspaper today," he said, waving a copy of the *Abbey Park Chronicle* at her.

"Oh!" Isla said. "We've been checking the

paper every day. I didn't think it came out on
Sunday."

She dragged an old bucket over to the
fence and climbed up to have a look.

Local Heroes, the headline said, *by Sally
Smithers.*

"There's a picture of Mum with Poppy and
Roo!" Isla said excitedly.

Abbey Park Vets is not your average local veterinary surgery, Isla read. *Veterinarian Lucy Bramwell and veterinary nurse Sarah Palmer work tirelessly to heal the animals at Abbey Park, often opening late or on weekends. When I met with Sarah Palmer at her home to talk about the good work she does, I found something even more impressive.*

There was a picture of Poppy with her paw in the air with the caption: *Poppy Palmer – Wonder Cat!* Isla read on eagerly. *It's not unusual to find a veterinary nurse who really cares about the welfare of the animals they treat, but Ms Palmer and her family have gone a little bit further. When they discovered that the local cat sanctuary was full – sadly, a common occurrence – they took action, giving Poppy a home with them. They soon discovered that Poppy is no ordinary cat.*

"*She can talk,*" *Milo Palmer told me.* "*Not real words, but if you say something to her, she will answer you with a meow. She can give you a high-five as well. She's brilliant!*"

This heart-warming story doesn't end there. When a young cat was cruelly abandoned at the veterinary surgery, the Palmers took him in as well. This is certainly one extraordinary family.

Isla beamed at Sam. The article made them all sound wonderful. It went on to include a short interview with Lucy, followed by profiles of some of the cats at the local sanctuary who needed a home. They'd even included the details of Poppy's videos on Tilda's YouTube channel.

Isla re-read the article a few more times, then noticed that something was missing. "Oh no," she groaned.

"What's wrong?" Sam asked. "I thought

it was brilliant!"

"It is," Isla said. "But look – Tilda is going to be so disappointed."

She pointed to the family photograph – Milo and Isla were in the middle, with Gran and Mum next to them holding Poppy and Roo. Even Sally Smithers was in the background. But all you could see of Tilda was a bit of her arm and one foot at the very edge of the picture.

"Well, I think it's a lovely article," Gran said as they gathered around the newspaper that evening.

"Are we famous now?" Milo asked.

"I don't think so." Mum smiled. "I'm glad they mentioned the sanctuary, though.

Hopefully some of the cats will be rehomed."

Mum and Gran settled themselves in front of the television with strict instructions not to be disturbed unless there was a dire emergency. Isla went to call Grace and tell her about the article, but there was no answer, so she headed upstairs to send an email instead.

"Don't come in!" Tilda shouted as Isla went to get the laptop from their room.

"Are you still upset about the article?" Isla called.

"No!" Tilda squeaked.

Isla tried the door handle but the door wouldn't budge. "Why won't you let me in?" she said. "It's my room, too!"

Tilda gave a huff and the door flew open.

"Are you very disappointed?" Isla asked.

Tilda sighed. "A bit, especially as I'd

told all my friends about it. But look at the number of views Poppy's had."

Isla pulled up Poppy's YouTube video on the laptop and gasped. There had been almost five hundred views.

"It must be because of the article," Tilda said.

Isla smiled. If one article could get this many people to watch Poppy's video, maybe some of them would look at the cats on the sanctuary website, too, and think about giving one a forever home.

Her thoughts were interrupted by a sudden loud knock at the front door.

"I'll go," said Tilda. "Don't touch the laptop, I'm still using it."

As Tilda bounded downstairs, Isla closed the YouTube window and peered at the screen, trying to work out what Tilda had been up to – surely she wasn't still doing her homework?

A minute later Tilda was back, looking pale. "You'd better come and see this."

Isla followed her downstairs. A soggy cardboard box was sitting in the porch with a smudged label that said *The Palmers* stuck to the top. Isla lifted the flap and gasped. Inside, curled into a shivery ball and making the most terrible mewing sound that Isla had ever heard, was a beautiful tabby cat.

Chapter
Nine

Isla yelled for Mum as she tried to soothe the cat with gentle shushing noises. The article had been supposed to encourage people to adopt cats from the local sanctuary rather than drop unwanted ones at their house. And something was bugging Isla – how had the cat's owner known where they lived? Maybe they'd recognized Mum from the vets, or Milo … or Isla from school.

Usually Isla would have been over the moon about another cat to look after, but this time – as another pained cry came from the box – she felt a little scared. Mum took one look and carefully carried the box into the kitchen, with Isla and Tilda hurrying after her.

"What's wrong with it?" Tilda asked, her face pale.

"I'm not sure." Mum frowned. "I'm going to give Lucy a call. You two stay here."

Isla covered the cat with a blanket and stroked its head to try to calm it down. Poppy weaved in and out of Isla's legs, while Roo hid behind the bin. Isla was glad that Milo was already in bed. Tilda poured some water into a saucer, and placed it in front of the cat, but it ignored the water and mewed even louder.

Isla noticed a soggy note taped to the side of the box. She pulled it off, reading out loud: *"This is Benny. Please take care of him."* She turned the note over, but it was blank. No clues as to where Benny had come from or why he'd been left on their doorstep.

After a lot of stroking and gentle cooing, Benny seemed to calm down. He lapped at the saucer, leaving little splashes of water across his nose.

Mum reappeared clutching the phone. "Lucy's out so I've left a message for her to call." She glanced at Benny. "He looks a bit better. Maybe he was just cold and scared. You two should go to bed, it's getting late. Gran's already gone up."

"But we can't leave him alone all night!" said Isla. "What happens if he's really ill?"

"I'll stay with him until I hear back from Lucy. Hopefully the cat sanctuary will be able to take him in the morning. Two cats are more than enough for us to cope with."

"Why do you think someone left Benny at *our* house?" Isla wondered again out loud as she and Tilda plodded up the stairs. "It can't just be a coincidence."

"How should I know?" Tilda snapped.

"I was only saying," Isla muttered.

"Sorry," Tilda whispered as they tiptoed

past Milo's room. "I'm just worried."

"Me, too," Isla said. "Do you think he'll be OK?"

After a long pause, Tilda replied in a small voice. "I hope so."

Isla tried to sleep, but every time she closed her eyes all she could see was Benny in his soggy box, mewing pitifully. Mum had come up to tell them that Lucy was going to pop by in the morning, but it didn't make her feel any better. She could hear Benny's weak mewing coming from downstairs, and as it was clear she was going to be awake all night, she decided to keep him company.

She dragged her duvet off her bed, trying not to wake Tilda, and crept past Gran's room. Her door was open and small snoring sounds came from inside. Poppy was curled up on the end of the bed, and for a second Isla felt a small pang of jealousy, wishing that Roo was allowed to sleep with her. As soon as Poppy saw Isla, she jumped silently down from the bed and followed after her, seeming to sense that she was a little afraid.

They padded down the stairs, with Isla making sure to avoid the creaky step at the bottom. When she got to the kitchen, she was surprised to find Mum already there, sitting on the floor in her pyjamas and whispering to Benny. "That's it, you'll be OK. I'm here."

Isla's hands flew to her mouth. "What's happening?"

The mewing got louder. Isla tried to move closer, but her feet wouldn't budge. She couldn't bear to see Benny in so much pain. She burst into tears – it was like losing Grandad all over again.

Mum hurried over and hugged Isla. "Shh, it's all right, honey. She's going to be OK, I promise."

"Really?" Isla sniffed. "Wait – she?"

Mum smiled. "It turns out that Benny's not a boy after all, and she's going to be better than OK. Look, Isla."

Isla crept forward, squeezing Mum's hand tightly. Benny was still mewing loudly from beneath the kitchen table, where she was lying on top of lots of old newspapers. There was a small movement under Benny's tail and something tiny and black wriggled out. One tiny pink nose snuffled at Benny's stomach, then another and another.

"Kittens!" Isla squealed, crouching down. "She's had kittens."

Mum grinned. "She wasn't ill – she was about to give birth. I had my suspicions, so thought I'd better stay up with her."

She nodded at the duvet in Isla's hand and at Poppy, who was weaving around Isla's legs purring loudly. "Looks like you two had the same idea."

Isla picked up Poppy and hugged her tightly. "Look, Poppy! More friends for you to play with."

Mum groaned. "What are we going to do with all these cats? We've turned the house into a cat sanctuary!"

Isla counted the kittens. There were four in total, a mixture of browns and whites and blacks like their tabby mother. They were covered in a wet, sticky goo that Benny licked off as they snuggled against her.

"We could keep them?" Isla said hopefully.

"We're going to have to keep them for at least eight weeks," Mum said. "Until they're ready to leave their mother. I don't think it's fair to take them to the cat sanctuary now. I'm not sure they'd have room for them anyway." She sighed. "Not that we really have room here, either."

"We'll make room," Isla said. "I'll make them a special space in the conservatory in the morning."

Mum gave Isla a hug. "You need to get some sleep, Isla Palmer. And besides, we need to give Benny space to bond with her babies. Lucy will take a look at the kittens in the morning to make sure they're all healthy, but we're going to have our hands full for a while. I'm going to need my best cat expert to help me out."

Isla grinned. She said goodnight to Benny and the kittens and went back to bed, depositing Poppy back on Gran's bed as she passed. There was no way Isla could sleep now, though. She was far too excited about the new arrivals. She'd never seen newborn kittens before. She opened the laptop to write an email to Grace and Ayesha. A strange icon she'd never seen before flashed in the corner of the screen. Isla clicked on it and a brightly coloured website popped up.

"That was supposed to be a surprise," Tilda groaned sleepily.

"Sorry!" Isla said, quickly shutting the laptop. "I wasn't snooping – not on purpose."

"It's something I've been working on for Poppy and Gran … and for you."

"For me?" Isla asked, puzzled.

Tilda yawned and sat up. "See for yourself."

Isla looked at the web page and gasped. In bold pink, loopy writing was the heading *A Cat's Tale*. Tilda had created an entire website all about Poppy – how she had come to the Palmers' house, about her accident and how they'd been helping her get back on her feet. There was a link to the newspaper article and a post written by Tilda about how amazing Poppy was and all the clever things she could do, with videos of her giving Tilda's friends high-fives and meowing to Gran as she chatted to her. Roo had his own page, too, which was mostly cute pictures and a video of him chasing Milo around the garden. There was also a story about a homeless cat.

Isla started to read it, then paused. "That's my story! The one I wrote about Poppy."

Tilda nodded and bit her lip. "Is that OK? You left your notebook out and I read it. It's so brilliant I had to use it. I *was* going to ask you," she said hurriedly, "but I wanted the website to be a surprise. I'm not the only one who thinks it's brilliant – take a look."

Isla was stunned. People had read her story and left comments about how much they'd enjoyed it.

"It's gone crazy, Isla," Tilda said excitedly. "You won't believe how many people have visited the blog and watched the videos. I can barely keep up with it all!"

"It's amazing!" Isla breathed. "Did you do this all by yourself?"

Tilda nodded again. "I've been doing a coding course at school. Mr Mills wanted us to choose a theme for a website, and Poppy seemed like the perfect answer. He didn't actually ask us to build a website, but I thought I'd give it a try. It's taken me *ages*, but I'm really pleased with it. I was going to show you all tomorrow, but –" she paused – "I think Mum's going to be a bit upset with me."

"Why?" Isla asked.

"Because … I think *A Cat's Tale* might be the reason someone left Benny on our doorstep," Tilda said, showing Isla the *contact us* page, which had their address on it.

"Oh!" Isla said.

"I only put it there in case anyone wanted to send Poppy fan mail or something," Tilda said quickly. "Mum's been getting so fed up with the cats, I don't know how she's going to cope with another one…" She paused, seeing the look on Isla's face. "Why are you looking at me like that?"

Isla smiled. "Something amazing has happened!"

Chapter
Ten

"I still can't believe you didn't wake me
up as soon as they were born!" Tilda said
a week later as she filmed the kittens. "I
could have made a birth video."

"Ugh, gross!" giggled Milo, pulling a face
at Sam who had come over to see the kittens.

Tilda rolled her eyes at her little brother.
"How's your post coming along, Isla?"

"I'm just about to write up Week Two,"
Isla replied, reaching for her notebook.

Tilda had asked Isla to write something about the kittens for the website. Isla was keeping a diary of everything the kittens did, partly because she thought it would be a great way to inform other people about how to look after newborn kittens and partly simply because people loved kittens. Tilda thought it would make the website even more popular.

Mum and Gran had been impressed with how professional the website looked. None of them – Isla included – had realized that Tilda was a coding wizard. At least now Isla knew why Tilda had been spending so much time on her laptop. And Mum was pleased because she thought it would generate interest in the kittens when it came to rehoming them. She had made Tilda remove their address though, and had given her a lecture about internet safety.

Isla took out her pen and began scribbling down everything she'd discovered so far.

Kitten Diaries – Week Two

What to expect when your cat has kittens, and things that might happen that you would never expect to expect:

Isla frowned as she re-read what she'd written – she'd think of a better title later.

1. Kittens don't open their eyes until they are almost two weeks old, so don't worry about them being born with their eyes closed.

2. When they finally do open their eyes, they will be blue, but they won't stay that way...

Probably, Isla added. She'd read that in one of the cat books she'd checked out of the library, but she made a note to double check with Lucy.

3. Kittens can't walk until they are three or four weeks old, but they can scoot along using their paws.

The scooting was the cutest thing Isla had ever seen. Tilda had uploaded a kitten video to YouTube and it was nearly as popular as Poppy's first video. There were lots of requests from people asking to give the kittens a home. Isla hoped that Mum would never read the comments because she didn't want the kittens to ever leave.

Isla had made the kittens an enclosure from an old wooden drawer with high cardboard sides, so that the kittens couldn't jump out or escape. They'd had to get another litter tray, much to Tilda's disgust, but the kittens were so cute, Isla didn't mind dealing with the poop.

Isla had moved Benny's cat bed next to the kitten enclosure so that she could keep an eye on them as well. Benny had settled in surprising quickly, and was even more huggable than Poppy. The moment anyone sat down, Benny leaped on to their lap, purring loudly.

Milo had decorated the cardboard walls with pictures of the kittens as superheroes, wearing capes and masks.

"This is Captain Snuggles," Milo told Sam. He pointed to a kitten as it half-rolled, half-crawled over its sister and brothers. "The small one with the black patch over his eye is Fluffboy."

Isla thought it would have been cleverer to give him a pirate name like Captain Patch or One-Eyed Jack, but Milo had insisted on Fluffboy.

"The girl kitten is Lady Mewington," Milo continued.

"How do you know which ones are girls and which are boys?" Sam asked.

"It's obvious!" said Milo matter-of-factly.

"Lucy told us," Isla said, picking up the kitten to give her a cuddle.

Milo pulled a face at Isla when Sam wasn't looking.

"And this one," Milo continued, picking up the biggest of the litter, who gave a tiny meow, "is Dynamo!"

Sam glanced at Isla for an explanation and she shrugged. "Mum said he could name them until we find them new homes. It does make it a bit easier to keep track of them."

Milo tugged on Sam's arm to get his attention. "This is the latest edition of the *Super Cats* comic. Do you want to buy a copy?" He showed Sam a handful of comics that Mum had photocopied for him at work.

Sam flicked through Milo's home-made comic. It was covered in scribbled drawings of the kittens wearing various superhero outfits and saving the world from the evil Dr Dogg. Isla thought it was actually pretty good, even though it was a bit hard to read Milo's handwriting. Tilda was going to scan and upload it to the website so Milo wouldn't feel left out.

"It's only two pages long because it took

me ages to colour in," Milo explained, "but I'll let you have it for the special price of one pound."

Sam raised his eyebrows and dug around in his pocket, producing a fifty pence piece and a couple of chewy fruit sweets. Milo grabbed the coin and the sweets, and shoved the comic in Sam's face. "That'll do!"

There was a knock at the front door.

"That'll be Grace and Ayesha," said Isla, putting Lady Mewington back in the box. "They're coming to see the kittens, too!"

As soon as she opened the door she was met by a sea of faces.

"What's going on?" she gaped.

Behind Grace and Ayesha was a group of boys. Isla wasn't sure she recognized them until Sam called out "Hi!" from behind her, and she realized they were the ones who had laughed at her in the park.

"We bumped into them on the way over," Ayesha said, looking a bit guilty. "Mark and Tamar are my brother's friends from school, and this is Matt and Joe. I *might* have told them about the kittens and invited them along."

Mark gave Isla a grin. "Sam's mum said he was here, too."

"Quick, Sam, hide!" Isla teased as she ushered them indoors. "You don't want your friends to see you with a girl."

Sam's cheeks turned pink.

"What's all this?" Gran asked as they trooped past the kitchen to the conservatory.

"Visitors to see the kittens," Isla said.

"Does your mum know about this?" Gran asked uncertainly.

"She did say she wanted the kittens gone

as soon as they were old enough," Tilda said, coming to see what all the noise was about. "What better way than to let people try before they buy?"

Isla introduced the kittens to everyone and Milo tried to sell more copies of his comic. Grace took a selfie with the kittens in the background. "If this doesn't convince my dad to let me have a cat, I don't know what will. They're so adorable!"

Ayesha nodded in agreement as Tamar snuggled with Benny, who had settled on his lap. "Even the boys can't resist them!"

Isla frowned. "The kittens aren't for sale."

"Not yet," Tilda replied, glancing at Isla. "But we can't keep them forever and school starts in a week. Who's going to look after them then?"

Isla's heart sank. She had been so caught up with the cats that she hadn't stopped to consider what might happen when Mum was at work and they were all at school.

Gran appeared with a huge plate of brownies, which her friends devoured in seconds.

"You'll still be here though, won't you, Gran?" Isla asked. "When we go back to school?"

"I'm not sure, Isla," Gran said. "I've been

here for longer than I'd planned as it is. I'm going to have to talk with your mum."

She went off to refill the plate. Isla tried to join in with her friends as they took photos of the kittens and laughed and joked around, but could only force a small smile that she didn't really feel inside. Everything was changing too quickly – new school, new friends, new homes for the kittens. Isla didn't know what she would do if Gran decided to leave as well.

That evening, Mum got an emergency call from work. With Gran out at Zumba, she left Tilda in charge, with instructions not to answer the door and to have Milo in bed by eight o'clock.

Isla was in the lounge with Benny asleep on her lap, trying to finish her kitten diary entry for that day. Poppy and Roo were curled up together on the other end of the sofa. Roo seemed to think that Poppy was his mother. Isla was just writing about how the kittens had already doubled in size, when there was a loud bang from the kitchen.

"Tilda?" she called quietly, not wanting to disturb Benny. "Milo?"

"Help!" Milo squeaked.

Isla put Benny down next to Poppy and Roo and rushed to the kitchen. Milo was standing in the centre of the room surrounded by a billowy white cloud of flour that coated his hair, his face and his clothes. But that wasn't the worst of it – the kitchen counters were covered in broken eggs and puddles of coloured icing. A bottle of milk had been knocked over and was slowly pouring on to the floor and mixing with the flour to make a gloopy mess.

"What have you done?" Isla whispered.

Milo looked like he was about to cry. "I wanted to make a cake to surprise Gran," he wailed, "but it went a bit wrong."

Isla stared at the chaos. How could someone so small make so much mess in such a short amount of time?

"Just. Stand. Still!" she said, trying to mop up some of the milk with a tea towel but only spreading the mess further across the worktop.

"What's happened?" Tilda shouted, as she came charging in. She slipped on an egg yolk and flew across the room, sliding into the pancakey mixture on the floor.

"What is this stuff?" Tilda shrieked,

picking the gloop out of her hair and struggling to her feet.

As Isla explained what had happened she saw a small white lump squirming across the floor. "What's that?" she said, grabbing Tilda's arm.

"I wanted some company!" Milo cried, looking panic-stricken.

Isla watched open-mouthed as two more flour-covered lumps wriggled around in the mess. Benny appeared in the doorway and at once the floury lumps scooted over to her.

"The kittens!" Isla cried, as Benny licked each of them in turn.

Tilda picked up two of them and Isla scooped up the third, who turned out to be Lady Mewington. The tiny kitten had blue icing all over her paws and had left a trail of prints across the room.

"Where's Dynamo?" Isla said, frantically searching the floor for signs of the last kitten.

Milo pointed to a squiggly trail that had worked its way through the flour. They followed the path out into the hallway where it stopped suddenly at a pair of white trainers. The three of them looked up to find a flour-coated Dynamo purring happily in Mum's arms.

"What on earth is going on here?" she asked, pulling sprinkles out of Dynamo's fur.

"Milo wanted to make a cake," Isla said.

"And where were you?" Mum asked Tilda. "I left you in charge."

Tilda looked at the floor. "I'm sorry, I only went upstairs for a minute … or two."

Mum sighed, carrying Dynamo up to the bathroom along with his brothers and sister. "I'll clean up the kittens. You three can clear up the kitchen. I don't even want to see what it's like in there."

"I didn't mean to," Milo said glumly, as he brushed at the flour on the floor.

"I know." Isla sighed. "It was an accident. We're all just going to have to try harder to make sure the cats stay where they're supposed to."

"How are we going to do that?" Tilda asked. "Especially if Gran decides it's time to go – you heard what she said earlier."

"She can't leave yet, though!" Isla said, worried. "We can't look after the kittens when we go back to school, and … I love having Gran here."

Milo sniffed. "I don't want Gran to go!"

It felt like Gran had been living with them forever. She belonged with them, just like Poppy and Roo and the other cats. Isla couldn't imagine Gran not being around every day.

"We need to think of a way to keep everyone together," Tilda said. "Including the cats."

Isla grinned at her.

"What?" Tilda asked.

"You love ca-ats," Isla sang.

Milo joined in. "Tilda loves ca-ats, Tilda loves ca-ats."

Tilda laughed. "Well, maybe I've just got used to having the little furballs around, and anyway, I need them for my website. The more videos of the kittens I upload, the more hits I get. I'd have nothing to write about if we didn't have cats causing mischief every week."

"How are we going to do that, though?" Isla said. "Keep everyone together?"

"I'm not sure." Tilda frowned. "But I'm sure we can think of something."

Chapter Eleven

It was the day after the flour extravaganza, and Grace and Ayesha had come to see the kittens again, and to share their last-minute panics about starting secondary school.

"I wish I could keep one," Grace said sadly, cuddling Lady Mewington. Her mum had told her that she wasn't allowed to adopt one of Benny's kittens and she'd been sulking about it ever since.

"At least you can play with the cats here,"

Ayesha told her, frowning as she tried on her bright red blazer for the fifth time.

Isla nodded. "You can come over any time."

"Not for much longer," Grace sniffed. "School starts next week."

Isla wanted to say something to cheer Grace up, but she had the same worries. She didn't know how she was going to fit in school *and* looking after the cats. She was especially worried about the kittens. They were still too young to be left alone all day, and if Gran left, Mum would *have* to find them new homes.

"Isla," Mum said, hurrying into the conservatory. "Have you seen Benny?"

Isla shook her head slowly, realizing she hadn't seen Benny for a while. "I'll see if she's upstairs."

There was no sign of Benny upstairs and when Isla returned to the kitchen Mum was frantic. "I think she might have gone outside. Gran's checking the back garden, but there's no sign of her yet. We need to find her – quickly."

They'd been keeping Benny inside – partly because of the kittens and partly because she'd caught an infection after giving birth.

"I'll help," said Grace.

"Me, too," Ayesha agreed.

They hurried out of the front door and split up – Mum and Isla went in one direction, and Grace and Ayesha headed for the park. They yelled Benny's name, but there was no sign of her anywhere.

Isla paused suddenly. "What if she's gone back to her old house?" she asked. Cats had very good homing instincts. Isla had heard of cats walking for hundreds of miles to get back to their old homes when their owners had moved house.

"I'm sure she wouldn't leave her kittens," Mum said. "She's bonded with them really well. I'm sure she must be around here somewhere."

As they walked back to the house they saw a group of children huddled on the path that led to the back of their row of houses. Isla thought she recognized some of them from school.

"What's going on there?" Mum asked, hurrying over.

At the centre of the crowd they found Milo, holding out a jar filled with coins and a big sign that he'd stuck to the fence saying: *Hug a cat – 50p.*

Next to him
was a little girl
hugging Benny.
She had a huge
smile on her face.

"Milo!" Mum
shouted.

Isla had
never seen Mum
look so cross.

"I think you all need to go home now,"
Mum told the children. "Milo will return
your money tomorrow." She tried to take
Benny from the little girl, but the girl
shook her head.

"I've always wanted a cat," she wailed.
"But my mummy won't let me have one!"

Mum kneeled down in front of her and
sighed. "Benny's not feeling very well at

the moment, so she has to stay inside. But why don't you come over another day and Milo can show you our kittens? Check that it's OK with your mummy first, though."

The little girl nodded happily and handed Benny to Mum. Mum took Milo with her free hand and led him back to their garden. Gran was waiting anxiously with Poppy.

"What on earth were you doing, Milo?" Mum asked. "We've been searching for Benny everywhere. You know she's supposed to stay indoors."

Milo's lip wobbled. "I didn't take her far, and I was keeping a good eye on her. I was trying to make some money. I thought it would help to keep the kittens."

Mum gave Milo a hug. "I'm sorry, Milo. We can't keep the kittens. We have seven cats in the house. Seven! And five people.

It's just too much."

"We'll do better," Isla said, her eyes watering.

Milo nodded, but Mum shook her head. "Benny needs looking after, and the kittens need looking after. They're a lot of work. I look after animals all day long. When I get home I just want a bit of peace and quiet. I can't get into my own house any more because there are always people around to see the cats or sample Gran's cake!"

Gran frowned. "I'm going for a nap," she said. "I'm feeling very tired all of a sudden."

"Wait!" Mum called. "I didn't mean…"

As Mum went after Gran, Isla and her friends took Benny back to the conservatory.

Isla tried hard not to cry, but as she placed Benny with her sleepy kittens, the tears streamed down her face.

"Oh, Isla," said Grace, giving her friend a hug. "I know it's tough, but your mum's right – you can't have seven cats in the house."

"And at least you'll still have Poppy and Roo," said Ayesha.

Isla nodded. But if Gran decided to go home she'd take Poppy with her, and then they'd only have Roo. Isla could hardly bear the thought of it...

Gran stayed in her bedroom for the rest of the afternoon. Tilda was over at a friend's house and Mum made them something home-made for dinner for the first time in ages, but Gran didn't even come down for that. They ate in a gloomy silence – Mum worrying about Gran, Milo worrying about Benny, and Isla worrying about everything.

At bedtime, Isla found Mum sitting in Gran's usual chair, stroking Poppy. "Are you OK, Mum?"

Mum gave her a little smile. "Can I tell you a secret?"

Isla nodded.

"I do love cats as much as you, Isla."

"I know you do, Mum!" Isla said.

"I was so worried that we'd lost Benny today."

"Because of Millie?" Isla asked.

Mum nodded. "She was such a beautiful cat. Poppy reminds me of Millie so much. They have the same loving nature. I don't want to find new homes for the cats, but we can't go on like this. I've upset your gran as well, just when she was feeling better."

"I'm sure she'll be OK in the morning," Isla said.

Mum smiled. "I hope so."

Isla walked sadly up to bed, trying to think of a way she could make everyone happy again. As she passed her old bedroom she noticed that the door was slightly open, so she peered in. There was a suitcase on the bed and Gran was carefully folding her clothes and putting them inside.

Isla's heart dropped as she pushed the door open. "What are you doing?"

"Oh, Isla," Gran said. "I was going to wait until morning to tell you all."

Isla's heart pounded. "Tell us what?"

"It's time that Poppy and I went home. It's been lovely staying with you, but I think your mum needs her house back."

"But … you can't leave!" Isla cried. "The kittens need you! *We* need you! Everything is so much better with you here." Isla threw her arms around her gran. "Please don't leave."

Gran stroked Isla's hair. "I'm sorry, Isla, I've made up my mind. I really think it'd be for the best."

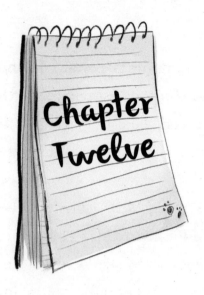

Chapter
Twelve

When Isla woke up the next morning, she forgot for a brief moment that Gran was leaving. Then it suddenly hit her and she slumped back on to her pillow with a sick feeling in her stomach. She didn't know how everything had gone so wrong. Last night she had managed to convince Gran to stay for one more day, but she wouldn't agree to staying any longer than that. Gran was leaving and taking Poppy with her, and there was nothing Isla could do about it.

Isla had had the best summer of her life with Gran and the cats moving in. She knew it was difficult for Mum working at the vets and then coming home to more cats, but she knew how much Mum loved them – even before she'd said so last night. She had seen it in her eyes when she looked at Poppy, and when she'd stayed up all night taking care of Benny, and even when she'd cleaned up the kittens after the flour fiasco. Isla needed a way to show her that things could be better. They *had* to find a way to convince Gran to stay.

Tilda came over and gave Isla a hug. "I didn't think she was really going to leave," she said sadly.

"Me neither." Isla sniffed. "I know we can make this better, Tilda. We just have to figure out how."

"Check this out!" said Milo, wandering into their room in his pyjamas, his hair sticking up as though he'd slept upside down. He held out the jar from the day before. It was packed with coins.

Tilda gave Isla a worried glance. "Where did you get all that from?"

"It's the money I made yesterday!" He grinned. "Mum says I have to give it back though, because we could get in trouble for asking people to pay to hug Benny, but I counted three times just to make sure, and there's nearly ten pounds."

"Wow," said Isla. "That's quite a lot of money just for hugging a cat."

"I know!" said Milo. "I got the idea after listening to Ayesha tell you about the cat café in Japan. The café sounded a bit like our house with all the cats and people always coming over to eat Gran's cakes."

Isla gasped. She jumped up, grabbing Milo by the shoulders. "That's it!" she said, kissing him on the head. "Milo! You are a genius!"

Milo rubbed his forehead, trying to get rid of any traces of Isla's kiss. "I am?"

Isla nodded and looked at Tilda.

"It might work," Tilda said thoughtfully.

"What might work?" asked Milo, confused.

Tilda gave Isla a warning look.

"Oh! Milo. I…" Isla looked to Tilda for help. He didn't know that Gran was leaving.

Tilda patted the bed beside her. Milo sat down, eyeing them both suspiciously. "What's the matter? Are the kittens OK?"

"The kittens are fine," Tilda said. "It's just that … Gran's decided to go home with Poppy." She tried to give Milo a hug, but he pulled away from her, shaking his head. He looked to Isla who nodded sadly.

"We knew she was going to go home eventually," Isla mumbled, trying not to cry in front of Milo. "But you've given me an idea of how we can convince Gran to stay *and* keep all of the cats."

She grabbed her notebook and scribbled down her plan as quickly as she could before she changed her mind. It was a risky idea and the chances of it working were slim, but they were desperate. Gran and Poppy *had* to stay.

"All of them?" Milo asked. "Even the kittens?"

"All of them!" Isla said. "We're going to need your help though, Milo."

Milo saluted. "At your service!"

Isla looked at her notebook where she'd written *Project Save the Cats and Gran!* then paused. They didn't have much time. They were going to need all the help they could get. She pulled the curtains open and peered out of the window into next door's garden. As she'd hoped, Sam was already up, kicking his football around. She was sure she could persuade him and his mates to help.

Isla grabbed Tilda's phone and called Grace and Ayesha, telling them to come over as soon as possible, and Tilda set to work on the website. Isla had heard Mum leave for work already, so they didn't have to worry about her being in the way.

"We need to find something to keep Gran occupied," Isla said.

"How about Mr Evans?" said Tilda. "I'll pop round as soon as I'm dressed."

Half an hour later, Mr Evans had turned up and whisked a surprised Gran away to help with his flowers. Five minutes after that, all the helpers gathered in the back garden.

"Everything has to be perfect!" Isla said, checking the details of their plan. "We've only got one chance to make this work, otherwise we lose Gran *and* the cats."

It was Milo and Ayesha's job to bake some cupcakes. Tilda had sent an email round, inviting everyone she could think of – Gran's new friends, her friends, Lucy, and Abbey Park Vets' regular visitors. Isla said that Sam's friends could come as long as they helped out and tried not to be too annoying.

Everyone had a job to do. They worked non-stop – painting, baking, decorating, rearranging furniture, right up to the very last minute. As Tilda heard the key in the lock, she gave Isla's hand a squeeze.

"This is it!" she squealed. "Is everything ready?"

Isla glanced around and nodded, giving Tilda a nervous grin. She took a deep breath as Mum walked through the door with Gran and Mr Evans not far behind.

"What's going on, Isla?" Mum asked, looking confused.

There were brightly coloured banners
hanging from the conservatory ceiling.
Tables inside and out were covered with
white tablecloths and flowers in bright
blue vases. Tilda had set up her iPod to
play some chilled-out background music
and there was a display of Ayesha and
Milo's slightly messy but delicious-looking

cupcakes. And best of all – people. Lots and lots of people.

The atmosphere was perfect. Everyone was laughing or chatting while Grace and Ayesha served them tea and cupcakes. The main attraction – the cats – were basking in all the attention, and it was clear how much joy they were bringing.

"What is all this?" Gran asked in awe.

"It's a cat café," Isla explained. "They have them in Japan – it's a place for people who love cats to go if they can't have a cat of their own. They get to spend time with a cup of tea and some cake and their favourite animal. The cats get lots of love and attention, and the best bit is how much people will pay."

Milo shook his jam jar filled with coins.

"I thought I told you to return that money." Mum frowned.

"I did!" Milo cried.

"This is all from today," Isla told her quickly. "People are happy to give a little money for some cake and tea and a cuddle with a kitten. If we opened a cat café, it would mean that the cats aren't alone all day, and we get a bit of money to help look after them. We could even do a cat adoption day every now and then to match people who are looking for a pet with cats looking for a home."

"You've got to admit, it's a clever idea," said Tilda, rescuing a kitten from Mum's handbag.

"I don't know, Isla," said Mum doubtfully. "It looks wonderful, but who's going to run it? I'm at work all week and you'll all be back at school on Monday."

Isla looked at Gran. "I was hoping…" She looked at Milo and Tilda, who nodded encouragingly. *"We* were hoping, that you would stay, Gran – you and Poppy – for good."

Gran glanced at Mum. "I'm not sure…"

"We need you, Gran!" Milo pleaded. "I can't make my cupcakes look as good as yours, and I don't think Mum will let me be head baker."

Mum laughed. "You've got that right."

"Would you want me to stay?" Gran asked Mum.

Mum hugged her tightly. "Of course I would! It's been so wonderful having you to stay. I couldn't have coped these last few weeks if you hadn't been here."

"Are we really doing this?" Tilda squealed. "Opening our own cat café? I could make a website – I've got the perfect idea for a logo."

"It's going to be a lot of work…" Mum said. "We'd have to do a lot more research first, and I'm not even sure we would be allowed to run a cat café from our home, but…"

"But…" Isla pressed, crossing her fingers behind her back.

"It's worth a try," Mum said. "If we do this together."

"Together!" Isla agreed.

Poppy meowed, batting a paw at them, and Mum gave her a hug. "Just look at what you've started, Poppy!"

"What do you think, Poppy?" Gran asked. "Do you think we should stay?"

Poppy waved her paw with a loud meow that Isla took as a yes. "That's settled, then." She grinned. "And I've thought of the perfect name for our cat café."

Isla watched Roo and the kittens rolling across the lawn with Sam and his friends chasing after them, and smiled.

"Poppy's Place."

Isla is over the moon that Mum has agreed to the idea of opening a cat café. Poppy's Place isn't only a solution to their houseful of cats, but a way of helping other homeless cats find a forever home, too.

But as they start on their plans, the 'to do' list just gets longer. There's so much to organize - the menu, the decorating, the website ... not to mention the task of creating a super-friendly space for all the cute and mischievous cats. As the grand opening looms, the family face a major setback. Will this be the end of Isla's dream?

KATRINA CHARMAN

Katrina lives in the middle of South East England with her husband and three daughters. She has wanted to be a children's writer ever since she was eleven, when she was set the task of writing an epilogue to Roald Dahl's *Matilda*. Her teacher thought her writing was good enough to send to Roald Dahl himself. Sadly, Katrina never got a reply, but the experience ignited her love of reading and writing.

Tweet Katrina: @katrina_charman

LUCY TRUMAN

Since graduating from Loughborough University
with a degree in Illustration, Lucy has become one
of the UK's leading commercial illustrators. Lucy
draws inspiration from popular culture, fashion and
all things vintage to create her fabulous artworks.
This, combined with her love of people-watching,
allows Lucy to create illustrations which encapsulate
aspirational everyday living.

Tweet Lucy: @iLucyT

Poppy's Place

Cat café or total CAT-ASTROPHE?

Join in the fun at
#POPPYSPLACE

Tweet @stripesbooks